Broken Wings

BOOKS BY KAHLIL GIBRAN IN THIS SERIES

Spirit Brides
The Storm
The Vision
The Beloved
Broken Wings

Broken Wings

A Novel

BY

KAHLIL GIBRAN

TRANSLATED BY JUAN R. I. COLE

WHITE CLOUD PRESS
ASHLAND, OREGON

01 00 99 98   5 4 3 2 1

Cover Illustration by Dennis James Martin
Printed in the United States of America

LIBRARY OF CONGRESS CATALOGING IN PUBLICATION DATA
Gibran, Kahlil, 1883-1931,
      [Ajniha al-mutakassirah. English]
      Broken wings : a novel / by Kahlil Gibran ; translated by
Juan R. I. Cole.
          p.   cm.
      ISBN 1-883991-03-X
      I. Cole, Juan Ricardo.   II. Title.
   PJ7826.I2A713   1998
   892.7'35--dc21   98-17734
                                                     CIP

Illustrations by Kahlil Gibran:
Crossed Open Embrace p. 7; Artist's sister, p. 19; The Flame, p. 58;
Mother and Child, p. 65; The Heavenly Mother, p. 81; The Spirit of
Light, p. 93; The Summit, p. 103; Self-portrait, back cover, Gifts of Mrs.
Mary Haskell Minis, in the collection of Telfair Academy of Arts and
Sciences, Savannah, Georgia.

CONTENTS

Author's Dedication

To the one who gazes at the sun with unblinking eyes, grasps fire with steady hands, and listens to the song of the "Universal" Soul amidst the clamor and uproar of the blind. To M.E.H. I dedicate this book.

Gibran

INTRODUCTION

Arab-American Kahlil Gibran (1883-1931) made his mark writing works of spiritual philosophy and prose poems on life's existential challenges, as exemplified in his classic, *The Prophet*, and in shorter pieces such as those collected in *The Vision*. Born in what is now Lebanon (at the time Ottoman Syria), he emigrated with his mother, brother, and sisters to Boston in 1895, as part of a wave of immigrants from the Eastern and Southern Mediterranean that transformed the United States between 1880 and 1924.

Gibran also was a short story writer and novelist, writing in the first two decades of the twentieth century, when those two genres were new to Arabic literature. (Gibran did not begin writing in English until 1918.) His 1906 *Spirit Brides* (*'Ará'is al-Murúj*) contained three short stories, among the first to appear in book form in Arabic. He followed that work with *Spirits Rebellious* (*al-Arwáh al-Mutamarridah*) in 1908. (Some of the stories in that volume were translated by John

Walbridge in his recent anthologies, *The Storm* and *The Beloved*.) Both collections of stories were published in New York by an Arab expatriate press, at a time when the young Gibran was attempting to establish himself as an avant-garde Symbolist painter in Boston.

Unlike his later, more ethereal aphorisms and prose poems, Gibran's short stories dealt openly with social problems and advocated what were, at the time, fairly radical solutions. He was especially critical of the treatment of women in the Arab world, of the treatment of the poor in Eastern and Western society, and of the hypocritical way Christian and Muslim religious authorities dealt with both.

These themes appear prominently in his 1912 novel, *Broken Wings* (*al-Ajnihahal-Mutakassirah*), published in New York. Set among Maronite Catholics in Beirut, the story follows a young man in love with Salma Karami, a lovely and pure young woman from a much wealthier class than he. Salma's father, bowing to pressure from the unscrupulous Bishop Ghalib, marries his daughter to the bishop's hard-hearted and avaricious nephew. Salma rebels by having an affair with the protagonist, with predictably tragic results.

Gibran uses this story to protest the practice of arranged marriage, advocating love and individual preference over patriarchy, wealth, and status. He decries what he sees as the corruption and coercive power of the church, praising individual conscience above the hypocritical, status quo institution. The book also hints at premarital sex and adultery, and seems to justify them with claims of romantic love over social convention. This was a radical stance for any writer in 1912, much less an Arab writer. That Gibran was expressing a philosophical conviction is suggested by his later writing in *The Prophet*: "If any of you would bring judgment on the unfaithful wife, let him also weigh the heart of her husband in scales, and measure his soul with measurements."

Broken Wings provoked great controversy in the Ottoman Empire and is said to have been banned there. Some readers have speculated that the story has its roots in an unhappy experience of Gibran's own youth, during the two years he spent at al-Hikmah College in Beirut, when he was interested in a daughter of the wealthy Dahir family but was not viewed as a suitable prospect by the family.

Beyond its enduring interest as a work of literature and social criticism by a major figure in American multiculturalism, Gibran's *Broken Wings* has a fair claim to being the first Arabic-language novel.

As with most premodern languages, classical Arabic literary forms did not include the novel. Arabic literature did boast the picaresque adventure cycle, including the stories of Sinbad the Sailor or the *Maqamat* (trickster-stories). Some nineteenth-century Arabic works of fiction attempted to revive these adventure stories in a new way, but these were not novels in the modern sense.

A few long prose works were serialized in Syrian newspapers in the late nineteenth century, straddling the space between the latter works and the modern novel. Long fiction appeared in Cairo by 1909, but scholars have yet to agree that the development and plot lines of such works were sufficient to identify them as "novels."

Muhammad Husayn Haykal's *Zaynab* appeared in Cairo in 1912—the story of a love affair between a notable and a peasant girl. One would have to know the month of publication for *Broken Wings* and for *Zaynab* to know which was the first published Arabic-language novel. But at the very least, *Broken Wings* deserves pride of place alongside *Zaynab*.

Whether it was the first Arabic novel or not, *Broken Wings* certainly innovated in the spiritual and moral spheres, bringing a neo-Romantic and symbolist sensibility to an Arabic literature that had mainly been characterized by a staid neo-Classicism. Gibran's lively evocation of young love, his portrait of a spirited and rebellious Arab woman, and his protest against the corruption and authoritarianism of his society's most prominent institutions all had an electrifying effect on his contemporaries. His lyrical prose poetry and uncompromising idealism still speak powerfully to us today.

Juan R. I. Cole
Ann Arbor, Michigan
Spring 1998

Broken Wings

PROLOGUE

I was 18 when love opened my eyes with its enchanted rays and touched my heart for the first time with its blazing fingertips. Salma Karama was the first woman to awaken my spirit with her charms. She led me toward the garden of lofty sentiments, where the days pass like dreams and the nights are spent like wedding feasts.

Salma Karama is the one who taught me, by means of her beauty, how to worship beauty, and showed me the enigmas of love by her tenderness. She is the one who chanted in my ears the line that begins the ode to the spiritual life.

What young man does not remember the first girl who, by her delicate grace, transformed his adolescent fantasies into terrifying wakefulness, wounding by her sweetness, lethally delectable? Who among us does not melt with yearning for that uncanny moment when, if he had been paying attention, he would have seen his entire being abruptly altered and transfigured, and his innermost depths expanded, enhanced, and deepened because of a delicious excitement—and this, despite all the heartache of keeping it a secret—an excitement that remained desirable even though attended by tears, longing, and sleeplessness.

Every young man has his Salma, who catches him unaware by materializing in the spring of his life, lending his solitude a poetic significance. Then she transforms the loneliness of his days into intimacy and the silence of his nights into songs.

I was baffled, torn between the impulses of nature and the teachings of books, when I heard love whisper with Salma's lips into the ears of my soul. My life had been empty, bleak, and barren, like Adam's stupor in paradise. Then I saw Salma standing before me like a pillar of light. Salma Karama was the Eve of this heart, filled with mysteries and wonders, and she was the one who made it understand the essence of this existence, who made it stand like a mirror before these apparitions. The first Eve forced

Adam's expulsion from paradise by her willfulness and his acquiescence, whereas Salma caused me to enter the garden of love and purity by her amiability and my willingness. But what befell the first man befell me as well, and the fiery broadsword that cast him out of paradise is like the blade that petrified me by the glint of its honed edge and that banished me from the garden of love before I had even disobeyed any warnings or tasted the fruit of good and evil.

Today, after the passage of gloomy years has blurred the outline of those days, nothing remains to me from that lovely dream save painful memories that flutter like unseen wings about my head, provoking sighs of grief in the innermost depths of my breast and distilling tears of sorrow and regret from my eyelids. And Salma—Salma the comely, the exquisite—has departed for what lies beyond the blue horizon, and no trace of her persists in this world save a choking agony in my heart and a marble tomb standing in the shadow of evergreen cypresses. That tomb and this heart are all that survive to tell the world of existence about Salma Karama. The silence that stands sentinel over graves does not divulge that closely guarded secret, which the gods concealed in the recesses of her coffin; and the branches that absorbed her bodily elements do not disclose, by their rustling, this reticent mystery. As for the anguish in this heart, it is what speaks, what now flows with the droplets of black ink, delineating the wraiths of that tragedy, which starred love, beauty, and death.

Friends of my youth, now dispersed through Beirut, if you pass by that graveyard near the stone pine forest, enter it noiselessly and walk slowly, lest your footfalls disturb the mortal remains of those laid to rest beneath the layers of earth. Stand in awe before Salma's tomb, greet for me the soil that embraces her body, and then mention me with a sigh, saying within yourselves, "Here were interred the hopes of that young man, whom the vicissitudes of time exiled overseas. Here his aspirations vanished, his joys abated, his tears dried up, and his smile faded. Among these mute graves his heartache grows along with the cypress and the willow. Above that tomb his spirit flitters every night, communing with memories, intoning with the ghosts of loneliness the dirges of sadness and misery, lamenting with the branches over a girl who was yesterday a spellbinding tune on the lips of life and today has become a silent mystery in the earth's bosom."

I implore you to swear, friends of my youth, by the women whom your hearts have loved, to place garlands on the grave of the woman whom my heart loved. Many a flower you encounter on forgotten tombs is like the dewdrops poured down by the eyelids of morning upon wilted rose petals.

WORDLESS SORROW

You remember, people, the dawn of youth with joy at recovering your impressions of it, and regret that it came to an end. But I remember it the way a man who has gained his freedom recalls the walls of his prison and the weight of his chains. You refer to those years that come between childhood and young adulthood as a golden era that scoffs at life's toil and anxieties and soars over the heads of exertion and worries, the way a bee floats above fetid swamps on its way to gardens in bloom. But I can think of no other description for the years of my adolescence than the time of hidden, wordless sorrows that took up residence in my heart, raging like a tempest within it, multiplying and growing. These sufferings found no aperture through which to escape into the world of knowledge until love entered therein, opening its gates and illumining its corners. Love freed my tongue so that it spoke, separated my eyelids so that they wept, and opened up my throat so that it sighed and complained.

You recall the fields, gardens, courtyards, and street corners that witnessed your games and heard the whisper of your innocence and I, too, call to mind those lovely places in northern Lebanon. No sooner than my eyes are closed to my present surroundings, do I see those valleys filled with awe and enchantment, those mountains full of glory and grandeur, striving toward the heights. No sooner than my ears are closed to the din of this meeting, do I hear the purling of brooks and the creaking of boughs. I long for these beautiful features that I now mention, just as a nursing child longs for its mother's arms. But they are precisely what torments my spirit, which is imprisoned in the unrelieved darkness of youth, the way a falcon is tormented by the bars of his cage when he sees his flock soaring free in the vast sky. This is what fills my breast with painful meditations and bitter thoughts, and weaves with the fingers of bewilderment and confusion a veil of melancholy and despair around my heart. I never went to the desert without returning from it depressed and ignorant of

the causes of my distress. I never gazed in the evening at the clouds, iridescent with the sun's rays, without feeling a ruinous dejection made worse because I could not grasp its implications. I never heard the warbling of the blackbird or the murmur of a stream without standing saddened by my ignorance of grief's origins.

They say that ignorance is the cradle of freedom, and freedom is the bed of comfort. This might be so in regard to those who are born dead and who live like cold, stiff corpses above the earth. But if blind ignorance dwells in the vicinity of a vital emotional life, it is crueler than hell and more bitter than death. The sensitive boy who feels much and knows little is the most wretched of all the creatures who bask in the light of the sun, for his soul is suspended between two opposing and horrific forces: the hidden power that carries him aloft to the clouds and shows him how beautiful things are from behind the mists of dreams; and a manifest power that binds him to the earth, covers his eyes with dust, and abandons him, lost and fearful, in the murky gloom.

Grief is a pair of hands that are soft to the touch, yet sinewy and powerful, which seize hearts and bedevil them by uniting them. Union is the viceroy of grief, just as it is the intimate friend of every spiritual movement. The soul of a boy suspended between the motive power of union and the influences of grief resembles a lily when it opens its petals. It quivers with the breeze, opens its heart to the rays of dawn, and contracts as the phantoms of evening pass. If the boy has no pastimes to distract his thoughts and no friends who share his interests, the life that stretches before him is like a constricting jail cell, in whose corners only spider webs can be seen and only the rustling of vermin can be heard.

As for the grief that pursued the days of my youth, it did not result from any dearth of pastimes on my part, for I had many. Nor did it ensue from a lack of friends, for I found them wherever I went. Rather, its origins lay in the traits and nature of my soul, which impelled me to be a loner and to seek union, and which snuffed out my former interest in games and hobbies and removed from my shoulders the wings of boyhood. Grief made me, before the universe, like a pool of water amid mountain peaks, which mirrors in its dour stillness their outlines, along with the colors of the clouds and the strokes of branches. But it finds no watercourse that would allow it to flow in lilting streams down to the sea.

That was what my life was, before I reached the age of 18, a year in my past that stands out like a towering mountain. For it stopped me in my tracks as I contemplated this world and showed me the paths of humanity, the plains of its interests, the steep byways of its toil, and the caves of its laws and customs.

In that year I was born for a second time. If tragedy does not ensnare a man, if affliction does not agitate him, if love does not lay him down in the cradle of dreams, then his life is like a blank, white page in the book of existence.

In that year I saw the angels of the heavens gazing at me through the eyes of a stunning woman, and that year I saw the demons of Gehenna, shrieking and racing through the breast of a criminal. For whoever cannot see angels and demons in the beautiful and hateful things of life, his heart remains remote from knowledge, and his soul is empty of emotion.

THE HAND OF DESTINY

I was in Beirut in the spring of that year, a spring that was filled with marvels. It was April, and the flowers and herbs had come up, adorning the gardens of the city like secrets whispered from the earth to the sky. Almond and apple trees were arrayed in fragrant gowns of white, looming among the houses like houris in ivory robes, whom nature had dispatched as brides for the sons of poetry and imagination.

Spring is beautiful everywhere, but it is more than beautiful in Syria. Spring is the spirit of an unknown god, hastening through the earth, and when it arrives in Syria it slackens its pace, glancing behind it, com-

muning with the spirits of the kings and prophets
that hover in those heavens, caroling with the Judean
streams the immortal songs of Solomon, hearkening
back with the cedars of Lebanon to memories of ancient splendor.

Beirut in the spring is more lovely than in other
seasons, for it is devoid of winter's mud and summer's
dust, subsisting between the rains of the former and
the heat of the latter like a comely young girl who
has bathed in the waters of a pool and then sat upon
its banks to dry her body in the rays of the sun.

On one of those days suffused with April's in-
ebriating breezes and welcoming smiles, I went to visit
a friend who lived in a house far from the din of the
crowd. While we spoke, sketching with our words
the outlines of our hopes and aspirations, there entered the room a splendid old man of about 65, whose
simple clothes and rugose features bespoke dignity
and gravity. I stood in respect and, before I could
shake his hand and greet him, my friend stepped forward and said, "This gentleman is Faris Effendi
Karama." Then he introduced me with effusive praise.

The elderly man stared at me for a moment, running the tips of his fingers across that high forehead
crowned by snow-white hair, as though he were trying to recover an old, mislaid image. Then he smiled
ebulliently and affectionately and drew near me, saying, "You are the son of an old and beloved friend, in

whose company I spent the springtime of my life. How happy I am to see you, and how I long to meet with your father through you."

I was touched by his words and felt a hidden pull that drew me close to him by means of an innate confidence, just as instinct guides a sparrow to its nest before a storm breaks. We sat with him and he regaled us with stories of his friendship with my father, recalling the days of youth they had spent together, reciting the stories of years that had expired and been buried in the heart of time and entombed in its breast. The old return in their thoughts to the days of their youth the way expatriates yearn for their birthplace; the old love to recount the tales of adolescence, just as poets love to read aloud their best verses. The old live by means of the spirit in the corners of the dusty past, for the present passes them by inattentively and the future appears to dwindle into the mists of closure and the gloom of the grave.

After an hour had passed in conversation and memories the way a branch's shadow passes over a lawn, Faris Karama stood up to take his leave. When I came near to say good-bye, he took my hand in his right and placed his left hand on my shoulder, saying, "I haven't seen your father for twenty years, but I hope I'll be able to compensate for his great distance by visiting you often."

I nodded, thanking him and bidding him fare-well, behaving in every way as a son ought toward his father's friend.

When Faris Karama had departed, I beseeched my friend for more information about him. He said in a cautious tone, "He's the only man I know in Beirut whom wealth has made virtuous and virtue has made rich. He is one of those rare individuals who come into this world and leave it without having ever caused grief to the soul of any creature. Such persons are usually themselves miserable and oppressed, for they are ignorant of the wiles that might deliver them from the plotting and malice of the people. Faris Karama has one daughter, who lives with him in a magnifi-cent mansion on the outskirts of the city, and she resembles him in character. No woman can rival her delicacy or beauty and she, too, is doomed to be mis-erable. Her father's immense wealth has brought her to the brink of a black and horrifying abyss."

As my friend pronounced these last words, signs of distress and regret appeared on his face. Then he added, "Faris Karama is an old man of noble heart and exalted character, but he is weak-willed. He is led like a blind man by the opinions of the people, and their ambitions reduce him to the silence of a mute. As for his daughter, she obediently submits herself to his feeble will, despite all the power and gifts of her magnificent spirit. That is the secret concealed behind the lives of father and daughter.

"This mystery was unraveled by a man who combines in his person ambition to be popular and a malicious cunning; and this man is an archbishop, whose vices proceed in the shadow of the Gospel and appear to the people as virtues. He is the religious authority in this land of religions and sects, feared by body and soul, and they all prostrate themselves before him, bowing the way livestock bend their necks before the butcher. This archbishop has a nephew in whom the elements of iniquity and wickedness struggle with one another, like scorpions and serpents wrestle in the corners of caves and swamps.

"The day is not far off when the archbishop will stand arrayed in the robes of his office, placing his nephew on his right and Faris Karama's daughter on his left, raising above their heads the marriage crown. He will bind, with the chains of priestcraft and sorcery, a pure body to a putrid corpse; joining, in the grip of a corrupt religious law, an astral spirit to an earthly essence; transplanting the heart of day into the breast of night. That is all I can say to you now about Faris Karama and his daughter, so don't ask me any more about them. Talking about a disaster helps bring it on, the way death is brought near by the fear of death."

My friend turned his face away and peered out the window into the void, as though probing for the secrets of days and nights among the particles of ether.

I stood and, as I was shaking his hand in farewell, I said to him, "Tomorrow I will visit Faris Karama, since I promised I would, out of respect for the memories of his friendship with my father."

The young man looked at me in amazement for a moment. His expression abruptly changed, as though my few simple words had revealed to him a new and bone-chilling thought. Then he looked into my eyes, with a long, odd gaze—a gaze of love, pity, and fear—the gaze of a prophet who sees in the inmost depths of spirits what spirits themselves do not know. His lips trembled slightly, but he said nothing. I left him and walked toward the door with scattered thoughts. Just before he turned his face away, I saw that his eyes were still following me with that strange look. I never understood its meaning until I freed my soul from the world of measurement and quantity and soared into the precincts of the Concourse on high, where hearts understand one another through glances and spirits grow by means of mutual understanding.

AT THE DOOR
OF THE TEMPLE

After a few days, when I grew tired of my solitude and my eyes wearied of focusing on the pages of frowning books, I took a carriage and asked for the house of Faris Karama. When we arrived at a pine forest popularly used to as a park, the coachman guided his horses away from the public thoroughfare and they trotted down a driveway shaded by willows. Along each side stood vegetation, latticed espaliers, and April blooms that smiled with mouths of ruby red, blue sapphire, and yellow gold.

After a moment, the carriage came to a halt before a freestanding house engulfed by a spacious garden wherein boughs intertwined and the air was perfumed by the fragrances of rose and jasmine.

I had taken only a few steps in that garden before Faris Karama appeared at the door of the house, coming outside to greet me. It appeared that the rumble of the carriage in that isolated spot had announced my approach. He greeted me cheerfully and led me hospitably into the house. Like a father who had been missing me, he sat me down next to him and conversed with me, asking about my past and my plans for the future. I answered him in that tone, suffused with the music of dreams and aspirations, which young persons affect before the waves of imagination cast them upon the shore of work, where they must toil and struggle. Youth possesses wings feathered with poetry and sinews rippling with vision, whereby it carries the young aloft, beyond the clouds. There they see the cosmos flooded with prismatic light rays like the colors of the rainbow and hear life chanting anthems of glory and majesty. But before long those lyrical wings are shredded by the storms of experience, and the plummet to the world of reality. The world of reality is a weird mirror, wherein men see themselves diminished and distorted.

At that moment there appeared between the velvety curtains at the doorway a girl wearing a plush, white silk dress. She walked toward me slowly, and I stood. Her father rose as well, and said, "This is my

daughter, Salma." After he spoke my name, he added, "That old friend whom the days had veiled from me has returned and manifested himself in the person of his son, so that I see my friend now, even though I don't see him."

The girl approached and looked into my eyes as though she wanted to make them speak to her about my reality, so that she might know the reasons for which I came to that place. She took my hand in a hand that rivaled the lily of the field in its whiteness and softness. At the touch of that palm I felt a strange, new emotion that resembled nothing so much as a poetic thought in the imagination of an author just as he begins to compose.

We all sat wordlessly, as though Salma had brought with her into that salon an exalted spirit that inspired silence and awe. Seeming to feel this, she turned to me and said, smiling, "Papa has often spoken to me of your father. He's told me over and over again the stories of their youth together. If your father has likewise recounted these events to you, then this is not really the first time we have met."

The elderly man delighted in the words of his daughter, and his expression turned cheerful. He said, "Salma is spiritual in regard to her desires and her religion. She sees all things swimming in the world of the soul."

In this way, Faris Karama resumed speaking to

me, with total concentration and friendliness, as though he had discovered in me an enchanted mystery that returned him on the wings of memory to the long-gone springtime of his life.

The aged man stared at me, seeking to summon the ghosts of his youth, while I contemplated him, musing on my own future. He cast his gaze over me the way the high, full branches of a tree cast their shelter, at the approach of the seasons, over a young sapling, full of calm determination and blind life: an old tree, firmly rooted, which has experienced the summer and winter of life and has stood before the squalls and gales of time; and a weak, supple sapling, which has seen nothing but spring and never shook save at the wafting of the dawn breeze.

As for Salma, she remained silent, looking in turn from me to her father as if she were reading in our faces the first chapter of life's story, and the last.

The day waned, its breaths sighing among those gardens, and the sun set, leaving golden kisses on the high peaks of Lebanon facing that house. Meanwhile, Faris Karama recited his stories, astonishing me; and I sang for him the songs of my youth, gladdening him. Salma sat near the window, watching at us with doleful eyes, motionless, listening to our conversation. She said nothing, as though she knew that beauty possesses a celestial language exalted above the sounds and syllables spoken by lip and tongue—an eternal language that embraces all the rhapsodies of human-kind, transforming them into voiceless feelings. In the same way, the music of brooks attracts the waters of the calm lake to their depths and renders them silent forever. Beauty is a mystery that our spirits compre-hend, in which they rejoice, and under the influence of which they grow. As for our thoughts, they stand before it perplexed, attempting to define and to in-carnate it in words, but they cannot. It is a torrent hidden from the eye, surging between the feelings of the beholder and the reality of the one beheld. True beauty lies in the rays that emanate from the holy of holies deep within the soul and shine beyond the body, just as life grows from the depths of a kernel, whereby a flower acquires color and fragrance. It lies in a complete mutual understanding between a man and a woman that is achieved in the wink of an eye. In a split second, it engenders a desire more sublime than any other, a spiritual attachment that we call love. Did my spirit understand that of Salma during that evening? Did our mutual understanding cause me to see her as the most beautiful woman under the sun? Or was it the intoxication of youth that set us to imagining unreal patterns and phantoms? Did my young manhood blind me, so that I imagined the rays in Salma's eyes, the sweetness of her mouth, the deli-cacy of her posture? Or did those rays, that sweetness, and that delicacy open my eyes to show me the joys and sorrows of love? I do not know. I do know that I felt an emotion I had never felt before, an unprecedented feeling that washed over my heart with a serenity that resembled the rustling of the spirit over the surface of the waters before the eons began. From that feeling was born my happiness and my misery, just as creatures were manifested and reincarnated time and again by the will of that spirit.

In that way the hour passed, the hour that joined me with Salma for the first time. It was the will of the heavens to liberate me, while I remained unaware, from slavery to confusion and youth, so that I might stride free in love's pageant. Love is the only freedom in this world, because it elevates the soul to a lofty station that cannot be attained by the laws and customs of human beings or conquered by the laws of nature.

When I rose to take my leave, Faris Karama came near to me and said, in a voice ringing with sincerity, "Now that you know the way to this house, you must come here with the same confidence that leads you to your own father's home. You must consider Salma and me to be your sister and father. Isn't that right, Salma?"

Salma nodded her agreement. Then she looked at me the way a lost stranger looks at a friend he recognizes.

The words Faris Karama spoke were the first in a melody that caused me to stand beside his daughter before the throne of love. It was the first movement of a heavenly symphony that ended as a dirge. It was a power that imbued our spirits with courage, so that we drew near to light and fire. It was a chalice from which we drank the elixir and the bitter lees.

I walked out, and the old man accompanied me to the edge of the garden. I said good-bye, my heart quivering within me the way a thirsty man's lips tremble upon touching the rim of the glass.

THE WHITE FLAME

April ended, and I was still visiting Faris Karama's house and seeing Salma. I sat before her in that garden and contemplated her charms, admiring her gifts, listening to the hush of her dejection, and feeling as though unseen hands were pulling me toward her. Every visit revealed to me some new aspect of her beauty, some sublime mystery of her soul, so that before my eyes she metamorphosed into a book, the lines of which I read, the verses of which I memorized, and the scores of which I sang. Nor could I ever reach its last page.

The woman to whom the gods grant a lovely soul along with a beautiful body is at once conspicuous and mysterious; we understand her through love and touch her with purity. When we attempt to depict her with words, she vanishes from our sight behind mists of bewilderment.

Salma Karama was lovely of soul and body, so how can I describe her to someone who does not know her? Can someone sitting in the shadow of the wings of death conceive of the warbling of the nightingale, the whisper of the rose, or the sighing of the brook? Can a prisoner weighed down with galling chains chase dawn breezes? Yet, is it not more difficult to remain silent than to speak? Will awe prevent me from giving you some idea of Salma in feeble words, despite my inability to sketch her reality with golden strokes? Someone starving, roaming in the desert does not refuse a crust of stale bread simply because heaven will not rain down manna and quail on him.

Salma possessed a slender body, and in her white, silky dresses she was like a moonbeam shining through a window. Her movements were slow and measured, like the music of Isfahan; her voice was low and dulcet, often interrupted by sighs, and it flowed from her cerise lips the way droplets of dew fall from the crowns of flowers shaken by a wind. Her face—who, I wonder, could portray the face of Salma Karama? With what words can I sketch a face that is forlorn and serene, concealed and yet not concealed by a yellow, diaphanous veil? In what language can I speak of features that every moment announce a secret of the soul and remind those gazing upon them of a spiritual realm remote from this world?

The beauty in Salma's visage was not based on the human criteria of beauty. Rather, it was uncanny, like a fantasy, a vision, or an exalted thought—incomparable and undefinable. No artist's brush could capture it, no sculptor's marble could incarnate it. Salma's beauty did not lie in her golden hair but in the halo of purity that enveloped it. It did not lie in her large eyes but in the light emanating from them, not in her rosy lips but in the nectar that flowed over them, not in her ivory neck but in the way it leaned forward slightly. Salma's beauty did not lie in the perfection of her body but in the nobility of her spirit, which resembled a white, blazing flame soaring between the earth and infinity. Salma's beauty was a sort of poetic genius, such as you witness in sublime odes and drawings and in immortal music. And the friends of genius are miserable, for no matter how high their spirits ascend, they remain encompassed in tears.

Salma was thoughtful and taciturn. But her silence was itself a sort of music, which transported those sitting with her to the arena of distant dreams, making them listen to the beating of their own hearts and causing them to see their imaginings and emotions standing before their eyes.

The one trait that suffused Salma's character was a profound, wounding sorrow. She wore her sadness as a spiritual badge, which made her body's charms all the more daunting and remarkable. The rays of her soul shone from behind that doleful web the way a blossoming tree rises behind the morning mists. Sorrow established a link of commonality between Salma and me, for we saw in each other's expressions what our own hearts felt, and heard in each other's voices an echo of the secrets concealed in our breasts. It was as though a goddess had fashioned each of us as half of the other, so that a pure combination of we two resulted in a whole person, while remaining separated caused each of us to feel a painful deficiency in our spirits.

A despondent, anguished soul finds repose in the company of another soul who shares in these feelings, just as two expatriates living in a foreign land delight in one another's society. Hearts that are brought together by the ache of despair are never estranged by the tinsel and bliss of gaiety, for the bonds of sorrow are stronger than the ties of joy and happiness. The love that cleanses the eyes with its tears remains pure, beautiful, and immortal.

THE TEMPEST

After a few days, Faris Karama invited me to an evening meal at his home. I went, my soul starving for that celestial bread the heavens had entrusted to Salma's hands; that spiritual crust we consume with the mouths of our hearts and which increases our hunger; that magical bread that was tasted by the Arab poet Qays, the Italian Dante, and the Greek Sappho, inflaming their breasts and melting their hearts; that bread into which the gods kneaded the sweetness of a kiss and the bitterness of tears, preparing it as fare for sensitive souls who, upon tasting it, awaken to the rapture within them, but who suffer torments as a result.

When I arrived at the house, I found Salma sitting on a wooden chair in a corner of the garden. She was leaning back, resting her head against the trunk of a tree, and in her white attire she looked like one of the spirit brides who stood guard over that place. I drew near to her wordlessly and sat nearby like an awestruck Zoroastrian before the sacred flame. When I tried to speak, I found my tongue tied up in knots and my lips frozen, so I communed with the silence. For a profound, infinite feeling loses something of its spiritual distinctiveness when it is incarnated in limiting words. But I felt that Salma was listening in the silence to the unceasing prayer of my heart, and seeing with her eyes the trembling, spectral form of my soul.

After a brief time, Faris Karama came into the garden and strolled toward us, greeting me as usual, extending his hand as though he wished to bless thereby the unseen mystery that bound my spirit to that of his daughter.

He said, smiling, "Let's go eat, my son. The food is waiting."

We rose and followed him. Salma was looking at me from beneath eyelids that had for their mascara kindness and affection—as though the phrase "my son" had awoken in her new, delectable emotions that became intertwined with her love for me, the way a child is entangled in its mother's arms.

We sat at the table, eating and drinking and conversing. We sat in that dining room enjoying the varied and savory dishes and aged wines, our spirits soaring in a world far distant from this earth, dreaming of future possibilities and preparing to stand before the ordeals and terrors to come. Our three souls diverged in their thoughts because of their differing aspirations in life, but our inmost souls were in accord, since their hearts were united in friendship and love—three frail innocents, who felt much but knew little. This is the tragedy played out regularly on the stage of the soul: splendid, honorable old man who loves his daughter and delights in nothing but her happiness; a young woman who sees the near future as still far away, who gazes toward it to descry the joys and hardships that will be her lot; and a young man with many visions and apprehensions who has not yet tasted the wine or the vinegar of life, who spreads his wings to soar into the skies of love and knowledge, but who is too weak to take flight. Three persons seated around an elegant table in a house secluded from the city, over which had settled the tranquility of dusk, on which the eyes of heaven were fixed. Three persons eating and drinking, in the bottoms of whose bowls and glasses fate had concealed gall and thistles.

We had not finished eating when one of the maids entered the room and addressed Faris Karama: "There's a man at the door who wants to see you, sir."

He asked, "Who is this man?"

"I think he is the servant of the archbishop, sir."

He fell silent for a moment, staring into the eyes of his daughter the way a prophet gazes at the firmament to discover its hidden secrets. Then he turned to the maid and said, "Tell him to come in."

The maid withdrew and shortly there appeared a man with a handlebar moustache, wearing gold-embroidered clothing. He bowed in greeting and addressed Faris Karama: "His excellency the archbishop has sent me in his private carriage to request that you accept the honor of coming to him. He wishes to discuss with you matters of some urgency."

The elderly man stood, his expression changing so that the cheerfulness on his face was veiled by worry and consternation. He walked over to me and said, in a voice full of charm and tenderness, "I hope I'll get back here in time to see you. Salma will find in you a companion whose conversation and spiritual songs can keep the loneliness of the night at bay." He turned to his daughter and added with a smile, "Isn't that right, Salma?"

The young woman nodded, her cheeks blushing slightly. In a voice that rivaled the reed flute in its delicacy, she said, "I'll make every effort to make our guest happy, father."

The old gentleman left, accompanied by the archbishop's man-in-waiting. Salma remained standing, gazing out the window toward the road until the carriage had disappeared behind the curtains of gloom, the rumbling of the wheels had faded in the distance, and stillness had absorbed the pounding of hooves. Then she sat before me on a chair embroidered in green silk. In her snowy outfit she looked like a lily raised up by morning winds in a grassy field.

Thus did heaven will it. I spent a night with Salma in that secluded house guarded by trees and drowned in silence, on whose grounds the phantoms of love, purity and beauty prowled.

As the moments passed we remained speechless, bewildered, lost in thought, each waiting for the other to begin. But is it speech that creates understanding between immaculate spirits? Is it the sounds and syllables issuing from the lips and tongue that bring together hearts and minds? Does not something exist that is more sublime than the words of the mouth and purer than the vibrations of the vocal cords? Is it not silence that bears the rays of one soul to another and conveys the whispering of one heart to another? Is it not silence that severs us from our own essences, so that we might soar in the boundless void of the spirit, drawing near to the Concourse on high, feeling that our bodies are nothing more than confining prisons and that this world is no better than a faraway place of exile?

Salma gazed at me, her eyes disclosing the se-

crets of her soul. She said, with an enchanting calm-
ness, "Come, let's go out to the garden and sit amid
the trees, so we can watch the moon rise over the
mountain."

I stood up obediently, but offered a small resistance. "Wouldn't it be better for us to stay here until
the moon rises and illumines the garden? Right now,
the darkness is concealing the trees and flowers, and
we won't be able to see a thing."

She said, "Perhaps the dark can veil trees and
flowers from the eye. But it can't hide love from the
soul."

She said these words in an eerie tone; then she
turned her eyes away and looked toward the window. I remained silent, pondering her words,
imagining the meaning of every syllable, and sketching for every meaning a reality. Then she turned and
stared toward me as though she regretted her words
and was attempting to retrieve them from my ears
with the bewitchment of her eyelashes. But their wiz-
ardry could not recover her words, which only
reiterated in the depths of my breast more clearly and
powerfully; those words stayed there, joined to my
heart, billowing with my emotions till the end of my
life.

Every great and beautiful thing in this world is
generated by a single thought or feeling within a human being. All the works of past generations that we

now witness were, before their appearance, secret thoughts in the intellect of a man or subtle emotions in the breast of a woman. The terrifying revolutions that have inundated the world with blood and fashioned liberty into an object of worship were born as imaginative ideas trembling among the folds of a single man's brain, who lived among thousands of other men. The ruinous wars that have toppled thrones and devastated kingdoms originated as notions pulsating in the head of an individual. The sublime teachings that altered the course of human life were poetic desires in the soul of a single man, sundered by his genius from his environment. One single idea raised the pyramids, and a lone emotion razed Troy; one conception founded the glory of Islam, and a single word demolished Alexandria's library.

One idea that comes to you in the still of the night carries you to glory or to madness. One glance from the corner of a woman's eye renders you the happiest of men, or the most wretched. One word issuing from the lips of a man enriches you after poverty, or impoverishes you after riches. One word pronounced by Salma Karama in that calm night brought me to a standstill between my past and future, the way a ship is suspended between the abyss of the sea and the layers of the atmosphere. A single, spiritual word roused me from the lethargy of youth and emptiness, setting my days on a new path toward the stage of love where life and death are played out.

We went out to the garden and strolled among the trees, feeling the invisible fingers of the breeze caress our faces while the soft forms of the flowers and grasses swayed at our feet. When we reached the jasmine shrub we sat, wordlessly, on the wooden bench and listened to nature's gentle breathing. Through the nectar of our sighs we discovered the mysteries in our breasts as we stood before the eyes of the firmament, which gazed at us from the periwinkle sky.

Abruptly, the moon rose from behind Mt. Sannin and flooded those hillocks and shores with its light. The villages on the slopes of the hills materialized as though blinked into being from nothingness. The whole of Lebanon appeared beneath those silver rays like a youth leaning on his arm and covered by a sheer veil that both hides and does not hide his members.

Lebanon is for Western poets an imaginary place, the reality of which faded with the passing of David, Solomon, and the prophets, just as the garden of Eden was hidden from view once Adam and Eve were expelled. It is a poetic expression—not the name of a mountain, an expression that symbolizes a soulful emotion and recalls images of cedar forests giving off their fragrance and incense, of brass and marble towers rising in glory and grandeur, and of gazelle herds prancing among hills and ravines. And I saw Lebanon that night as a poetic, imaginative thought, standing like a dream between two awakenings. Thus do things metamorphose before our eyes with the changes in our feelings, and thus do we picture things attired in enchantment and beauty, whereas these attributes exist only in our own minds.

Salma turned to me. The moonlight showered over her face, neck, and wrists, so that she looked like an ivory figurine carved by a devotee of Astarte, the goddess of beauty and love. She asked, "Why aren't you talking? Why don't you tell me about your past?"

I looked into her gleaming eyes and, like a mute who suddenly had found his voice, I answered, "Haven't you heard me speaking ever since we arrived in this place? Haven't you heard everything I've said since we came out to this garden? Your soul, which hears the whispering of flowers and the lilting of the silence, can hear the cry of my spirit and the clamor of my heart."

She covered her face with her hands, then said in a broken voice, "I heard you. . . . Yes, I heard you. I heard your voice crying out from the midst of the night and shouting frightfully from the heart of the day."

I had forgotten my past life, my being, everything. I no longer knew anything but Salma and felt nothing but her existence. I said quickly, "I heard you, Salma. I heard a grand, rejuvenating, wounding song that set the very atoms of the atmosphere to dancing, whose tremors shook the earth to its foundation."

Salma closed her eyes, and the ghost of a sad smile played over her crimson lips. "I know now that something exists more exalted than the heavens, deeper than the ocean, and more powerful than life, death, or time. I know now what I didn't know yesterday, what I didn't even dream."

From that instant on, Salma Karama became dearer than a friend, closer than a sister, more beloved than a lover. She became a lofty thought that followed my intellect about, a delicate feeling that embraced my heart, a lovely fantasy that dwelt in the vicinity of my soul.

How ignorant are those who imagine that love is born from long association and unbroken companionship. True love is the daughter of a spiritual understanding, and if that understanding is not achieved in a single moment, it will never be attained—not in a year, not in a whole century.

Salma raised her head and looked toward the faraway horizon, where the crenelations of Mt. Sannin meet heaven's hem. She said, "Yesterday, you were for me like a brother whom I could approach with confidence and whom I could sit beside in full view of my father. But now I feel something stronger and more exquisite than the affection of a sibling. I feel a strange emotion unconnected to any relationship, a surging emotion, both ominous and appealing, that fills my heart with sadness and rejoicing."

I answered, "Isn't this feeling that we fear, which makes us quiver when it passes through our breasts, a part of the universal law that sets the moon in orbit about the earth, the earth about the sun, and the sun and all that surrounds it about God?"

She put her hand on my head and ran her fingers through my hair. Her face was radiant, and tears glistened in her eyes the way dewdrops gleam on narcissus petals. She said, "Who would believe our story? Who would believe that in the hour between sunset and the rising of the moon we should have crossed the bridge and overcome the obstacles that lie between doubt and certainty? Who would accept that April, which brought us together for the first time, is the same month that admitted us to life's holiest of holies?"

While she spoke, her hand remained on my nodding head and, if at that moment I had had a choice, I would not have preferred the diadem of a king or a laurel crown to that silky hand playing with my hair. I replied, "People will not believe our story, because they do not know that love is the only flower that grows and flourishes without the cooperation of the seasons. But was it April that brought us together for the first time? Is it this hour that has admitted us to life's holiest of holies? Did not the hand of God unite our spirits before birth, making us captives of the days and nights? The life of a human being, Salma, does not begin in the womb, nor does it end before the grave. This unfathomed void that is filled with the rays of the moon and planets does not lack for spirits embracing in love and souls intertwined in under-standing."

Salma gently lifted her hand from my head, leav-ing a surge of electricity in the roots of my hair as the night breeze played with it. I enveloped her hand in mine, as a worshipper seeks blessings from the cloth over the altar, put it to my inflamed lips, then kissed it—long, deeply, silently, a kiss that would melt all the feelings in the human heart and awaken by its sweetness all the purity in the divine soul.

An hour passed, its every minute a year of pas-sion and love. The night's hush enfolded us, the moonbeams flooded over us, and the trees and flow-ers surrounded us. When we had attained the state that causes a person to forget everything but the real-ity of love, we heard hoofbeats and the rattle of carriage wheels speeding toward us. We awoke from that delicious trance and our wakefulness expelled us from the world of dreams into this world, which sub-sists between wonderment and drudgery. We realized that her elderly father had returned from the archbishop's mansion, and we strolled through the trees, awaiting his arrival.

The carriage reached the entrance to the garden, and Faris Karama descended and strode toward us, nodding his head, moving slowly, as though he were enervated and staggering under a heavy burden. He advanced toward Salma and put his hands on her shoulders, staring into her face for a long time, as though he feared that her form would fade from the sight of his weak eyes. Then tears flowed down his wrinkled cheeks and his lips quivered with a forlorn smile. He said, "Very soon, Salma, as is God's wont, you will be taken from this secluded house into the wide world, and this garden will long for your footsteps, and your father will become a stranger to you. Destiny has spoken, Salma, and may heaven bless and preserve you!"

Salma heard these words and her expression changed; she stared fixedly, as though she saw the apparition of death standing before her. She gasped, restless and in pain, like a bird that has fallen victim to a hunter and plummeted to earth shuddering with anguish. She cried out, in a voice broken with profound distress, "What are you saying? What do you mean? Where do you want to send me?"

She scrutinized him as though she wished to remove by her gaze the cloak that concealed the secrets

in his breast. A minute passed, heavy with silence
and its causes, resembling the wordless cry of the dead
in their tombs. At length she said with a sigh, "I understand, now . . . I know everything. The archbishop
has finished installing the bars in the cage that he has
prepared for this broken-winged bird. Is this your
will, Papa?"

He only heaved sighs in reply. Then he took her
into the house, rays of tenderness playing over his
distraught features. I continued to stand among the
trees, perplexity toying with my emotions the way
autumn gales trifle with dead leaves; then I followed
them into the salon. Lest I appear overly curious or
as someone who pries into personal affairs, I shook
the old man's hand in farewell. I looked at Salma the
way a drowning man fixes on a star shimmering in
the celestial dome. I left, without their being aware
that I had gone. But I had barely reached the outskirts of the garden when I heard the voice of the old
man calling. I turned and there he was, following me.
I returned to meet him, and when I approached him
he seized my hand and said in a quavering voice,
"Forgive me, my son. I've capped your night with
tears. But you will come to see me always, won't you?
Won't you visit me when this place is empty of everything but dismal old age? Vigorous youth doesn't
hang around with lazy old age, and the morning
doesn't meet evening. But you will come to me to

remind me of my boyhood, which I spent in the company of your father, to repeat in my ears the stories of a life to which I no longer belong, isn't that right? Won't you visit me when Salma leaves and I am left lonely and alone in this house, distant from all others?"

He said these last words in a low, broken voice. When I shook his hand in silence, I felt hot tears fall on my hand from his eyes. My soul flinched within me, and gentle, somber, filial feelings for him stirred in my breast and ascended like a gasp to my lips, then returned like groans to the inmost depths of my heart. When I lifted my head and he saw that his weeping had started the tears from my own eyelids, he leaned over and touched his trembling lips to my brow. Turning his face toward the door of the house, he said, "Good night . . . Good night, son."

One tear glinting on the wrinkled cheek of an old man is more affecting to the soul than all those shed by the eyes of the young.

The copious tears of youth gush from the corners of a full heart, whereas the tears of old age are the dregs of life that flow from the pupils, the remnants of life in a flagging body. The tears in the eyes of youth are like dewdrops on rose petals, but the tears on the face of old age are like the yellowed leaves of fall that are scattered by the winds when the winter of life approaches.

Faris Karama vanished behind the paneled door. I left the garden, Salma's voice still reverberating in my ears and her beauty walking like an apparition before my eyes. Her father's tears slowly dried on my hand. I walked out of that place the way Adam vacated paradise. But the Eve of my heart did not accompany me, to make the whole world a paradise. I left feeling that that night, wherein I was born again, was the night in which death's face loomed before me for the first time.

Thus, the sun rejuvenates the fields by its heat; and by its heat, it kills them.

LAKE OF FIRE

Everything a person does secretly in the dead of the night, the same person reveals openly in the light of day. The words our lips whisper in the silence become, unbeknownst to us, general conversation; and the deeds we attempt to hide today in the corners of our dwellings take form tomorrow and stand on the street corners.

Thus did the specters of night announce the intentions of Archbishop Paul Ghalib in meeting with Faris Karama, and thus did the particles of the atmosphere bear away his words to the quarters of the city so that they reached my ears.

The archbishop had not summoned Faris Karama to a meeting that moonlit night in order to consult with him about the affairs of the poor and needy, or to inform him of matters affecting widows and orphans. Rather, the archbishop had collected Faris Karama in a splendid private carriage to ask for his daughter Salma's hand in marriage to the son of his brother, Mansur Bey Ghalib.

Faris Karama was a wealthy man, possessing no heir save his daughter Salma. The archbishop had chosen her to be his nephew's wife, not for the beauty of her features or the nobility of her spirit, but because she was moneyed; her substantial fortune would guarantee the future of Mansur Bey and help establish his high status among the elite.

Religious leaders in the East do not content themselves with the glory and power they acquire for themselves. They do everything in their power to place their relatives in the forefront of the people, setting them up as tyrants and exploiters of others' abilities and wealth. The splendor of the emir passes by inheritance to his eldest son after his death. But the luster of the religious leader passes sideways down to his brother and nephew during his own life. Thus, the Christian bishop, the Muslim imam, and the Brahmin priest are all like octopuses, wrapping many tentacles about their prey and sucking the blood with numerous mouths.

When Archbishop Ghalib asked her father for
Salma's hand, the old man replied only with a profound silence and hot tears. What father would not
find it difficult to be separated from his daughter,
whether she were going to the house of his neighbor
or to the palace of a king? What man does not shud-
der in the depths of his soul when the law of nature
separates him from the daughter with whom he played
when she was a child, whom he reared as a girl, and
whom he kept company as a woman? The grief of
parents at the marriage of a daughter rivals their joy
at the nuptials of a son, for the latter acquires for the
family a new member, whereas the former robs it of
an old, beloved one. The old man answered the archbishop under duress, bowing before his will and
overcoming the resistance that welled up deep within
his soul.

Faris Karama had met the archbishop's nephew,
Mansur Bey, and had heard the people talk about him,
so he knew of Mansur Bey's coarseness, greed, and
corrupt morals. But what Christian can oppose a
bishop in Syria and remain well-regarded among the
believers? What man in the East can decline to obey
the leader of his religion and retain his honor among
the people? What eye can contend with an arrow and
avoid being gouged out, and what hand can combat a
sword without being cut? Suppose that this old man
were capable of opposing the Archbishop Ghalib, and

of blocking his ambitions. Will the reputation of his daughter be safe from malicious speculation and innuendo? Will her name remain unsullied by the filth of gossip and rumors? Are not all the grapes hanging out of reach sour in the religion of jackals?

In this way, destiny seized hold of Salma Karama and led her as an abject slave in the procession of miserable Eastern women. In this way, that noble spirit fell into a snare while it was yet soaring for the first time on the wings of love, in heavens suffused by the light of the moon and the fragrance of flowers.

In most places, the wealth of the parents causes hardship to the children. Those ample treasure chests that the energy of the father and the thrift of the mother fill up are transformed into dark, narrow prison cells for the heirs. That mighty deity whom the people worship in the form of money metamorphoses into a horrifying demon who tortures the people and kills the heart. Salma Karama was like many girls of her kind who are sacrificed at the altars of their fathers' fortunes and of their grooms' ambitions. Had Faris Karama not been a rich man, Salma would be alive today, rejoicing as we do in the light of the sun.

A week passed, during which love of Salma kept me company each night, singing songs of happiness for my ears and awakening me at dawn to show me the meaning of life and the secrets of existence. A sublime love that did not know the body because it was self-sufficient and did not pain the body because it subsisted within the spirit. A powerful desire that drowned my soul in contentment. A gnawing hunger that filled my heart with satiety. A feeling that gave birth to yearning but did not provoke it. A captivation that showed me the earth as a blessing and life as an exquisite dream. I walked through fields every morning, seeing in the awakening of nature the mystery of immortality. I sat on the seashore and listened to the waves perform ageless tunes, then walked through the streets of the city, finding in the faces of passersby and in the motions of workers the beauty of life and the pleasures of civilization.

Those days passed like phantoms and faded like mist, leaving no souvenirs behind for me but traumatic memories. The eyes through which I viewed the loveliness of spring and the awakening of the fields no longer gazed at anything but the wrath of the elements and the despair of winter. The soul that stood in awe before the vitality of the human race and the splendors of civilization no longer felt anything but the hardship of poverty and the wretchedness of the abject. How beautiful are the days of love and how honeyed their dreams; how bitter are the nights of heartache and how numerous their horrors!

At the end of that week, when the wine of my emotions had inebriated my soul, I strode one night to Salma Karama's house, that temple raised by beauty and consecrated by love, so that my soul might bow down there in prayer and my heart genuflect submissively. When I reached and entered that quiet garden, I felt the presence of a power that enticed and enraptured me, exiling me from this world and bringing me slowly to an ensorceled realm devoid of strife and conflict. Like a mystic whom heaven has attracted to a visionary state, I found myself walking among those intertwined trees and embracing flowers. When I neared the door of the house I looked around, and there was Salma sitting on that bench in the shade of the jasmine shrubs, just where the two of us had sat a week before on the night chosen by the gods as the beginning of my happiness and my misery. I approached her wordlessly. She neither moved nor spoke, as though she had known of my arrival before it occurred. When I sat next to her, she stared into my eyes for a minute, sighing long and deeply. Then she gazed at the distant horizon, where the portents of night dallied with day's last light. After a short time, filled with a magical stillness that ushered our souls into the procession of unseen spirits, Salma turned her face toward me and took my hand in her cold, trembling fingers.

In a voice like the moan of a starving person too feeble to speak, she said, "Look at my face, my friend. Look at it well, contemplate it at length, and read there all that you wish me to explain to you in words. Look at my face, darling. . . Look well, my brother."

I did look at her face, long and hard, and saw eyelids that had only a few days earlier been smiling and fluttering like the wings of a thrush, but which now were sunken, hardened, rimmed with the dark mascara of anguished and tormented imaginings. I looked at her complexion, which yesterday had been like white lily petals basking in the kisses of the sun, and found it sallow and withered, heavily veiled in despondency. I saw lips that had been as luscious as a chamomile flower, now dry like two withered roses that autumn had retained on the bush. I saw a neck that had been long like an ivory column, now bowed forward as though unable any longer to bear the weight of the thoughts roaming through her head.

I saw those painful transformations in Salma's features; I saw all of them, but they were in my eyes nothing but thin clouds veiling the moon, making it appear even more lovely and awe-inspiring. The expressions that reveal the secrets of one's spiritual essence endow the face with a beauty and comeliness, however disturbing and excruciating those secrets might be. As for those faces whose mien does not speak of the soul's riddles and innermost thoughts, they are not beautiful, no matter how symmetrical their lines or proportionate their features. Cups do not attract our lips until their crystal discloses the color of the wine. Salma Karama was, on the evening of that day, like a cup brimming over with celestial wine, in whose particles mingled the bitterness of life with the sweetness of the soul. She unwittingly represented the life of the Eastern woman, who departs from the house of her beloved father only to bend her neck beneath the yoke of her coarse husband, who leaves her mother's compassionate arms only to live in servitude to her pitiless mother-in-law.

I continued to stare into Salma's face, listening to her uneven breathing—silent, thoughtful, feeling, hurting with her and for her. I felt as though time had come to a standstill and existence had cloaked itself and vanished; I saw only two large eyes that stared into my inmost depths. I felt only a cold, shivering hand that grasped my own.

I did not awaken from that oblivion until I heard Salma say quietly, "Come, let's talk now. Let's try to imagine the future before it attacks us with its terrors. My father has gone to the house of the man who will be my companion till the grave. The man whom heaven chose as the cause of my existence went to meet the man whom the earth appointed as the lord of my coming days. In the heart of this city, right now the old man who was my companion all through my youth is meeting with the young man who will keep me company for what years remain to me; in this night father and fiancé have agreed on a date for the wedding, which will be all too near however distant they set it. How eerie this hour is, and how great its impact! On a night like tonight during the past week, in the shadow of this jasmine shrub, love embraced my spirit for the first time, even while destiny was scribbling the first word in the narrative of my future at the house of Archbishop Paul Ghalib. At this hour, while my father and my fiancé are sitting down to weave my wedding crown, I see you seated next to me. I feel your soul around me like a thirsty bird fluttering above a spring of water that is guarded by a ravenous, frightful serpent. How great this night is, and how deep its secrets!"

I imagined despair as an imperious phantasm that was choking our love, attempting to murder it in its cradle. "This bird will keep on hovering above that spring until thirst ravages it and destroys it, or until the horrendous snake seizes it, rips it apart, and devours it."

She replied, moved, her voice pulsating like silver strings: "No, no, my friend. Let this bird continue to live, let this nightingale warble till nightfall, until spring wanes, until the world ends and the eons cease. Do not silence him, for his voice revives me; do not clip his pinions, for their rustling dispels the clouds from my heart."

I whispered, sighing, "Thirst will kill him, Salma. And fear will put an end to him."

The words poured out urgently from her trembling lips: "The thirst of the spirit is greater than material quenching, and the soul's fear is more beloved than the self-assurance of the body. But listen, darling, listen well. I am standing right now at the threshold of a new life about which I know nothing. I'm like a blind woman feeling with her hands along the wall, afraid of stumbling. I'm a slave girl, and the wealth of my father has landed me in the middle of a slave auction, where some man has paid my price. I don't love that man, because I don't know him. You know that love and unfamiliarity don't mix. But I will learn to love him. I'll obey him and serve him and make him happy. I'll give him everything a weak woman can give a strong man.

"As for you, you're still in the springtime of your life. Life is a wide avenue that stretches before you, lined with flowers and blossoms. You'll enter the world's arena carrying your heart like a blazing torch. You'll think with freedom, and with freedom you will speak and act. For your father's straitened circumstances have not enslaved you, and his wealth is not such that it will drag you down to the slave market, where girls are bought and sold. You'll marry a young woman whom you choose for yourself, and you'll make a home for her in your heart before you'll bring her to live in your house. You'll share your thoughts with her before you share your days and nights."

She fell silent for a moment, to catch her breath, then added in a choked voice, "But have the paths of our lives parted here, taking you toward the glories of men and me toward the duties of women? Does the lovely dream end here, the exquisite reality scattered? Is this the way tumult drowns out the melody of the thrush, the winds scatter rose petals, and feet trample the wine glass? Is it in vain that this night has stood us together before the face of the moon, in vain that the spirit has brought us together in the shadow of this jasmine shrub? Were we speedily soaring toward the stars when our wings tired and cast us into the abyss? Did we surprise love in its sleep, so that it awoke, furious and intent on punishing us; or did our breaths stir up the night breezes, transforming them into a raging cyclone that ripped us to shreds and swept us away like dust into the chasm? No, a thousand times no! We disobeyed no warning, we tasted no fruit. So why must we leave that garden? We hatched no conspiracy, we never rebelled. So why have we plummeted into the inferno? The minutes that paired us are greater than centuries, and the ray that illumined our souls is mightier than any gloom. If the storm has separated us on the surface of this roiling sea, the waves will reunite us on that tranquil shore. If this life has slain us, that death will resurrect us.

"The heart of a woman doesn't change with time,

nor does it alter with the passing seasons. The heart of a woman struggles long, but does not die. The heart of a woman resembles a field on which human beings stage battles and massacres, uprooting trees, burning the underbrush, spattering the rocks with gore, sowing its earth with bones and skulls. But it abides, imperturbable, placid, self-assured; thereon spring remains spring, and autumn, autumn, till the end of time.

"Now, the matter is settled. So what can we do? Tell me what we can do, how we can part, when we shall meet? Should we consider love a guest, a stranger brought by the night and evicted by the morning? Should we reckon this soulful feeling a dream, brought on by sleep and banished by wakefulness? Raise your head so that I can see your eyes, my beloved. Open your lips so that I can hear your voice. Speak, tell me, talk with me: Will you remember our days together after the hurricane sinks my ship? Will you hear the rustling of my wings in the still of the night? Will you feel my breath surging over your face and neck? Will you listen to my sighs, ascending with an agony subdued by distress? Will you see my form advancing with the phantoms of night, fading with the mists of morn? Tell me, darling, tell me what will you be for me, after you were the light of my eyes, the song of my ears, the wing of my spirit—what will you be?"

I said, as my beloved wilted before my eyes, "I will be for you, Salma, however you want me to be for you."

"I want you to love me. I want you to love me till the end of my days. I want you to love me the way the poet loves his tenderest thoughts. I want you to remember me the way a traveler remembers a placid pool, in which he saw the image of his face before he drank from its waters. I want you to remember me the way a mother remembers a babe that died within her before it ever saw the light of day. I want you to think of me the way a compassionate king thinks of a prisoner who perished before the pardon could reach him. I want you to be for me a brother, a friend, a companion. I want you to visit my father when he is alone and console him in his solitude, for I will soon abandon him and go far away."

"I'll do all that, Salma. I'll make my spirit a cloak for your spirit, my heart a home for your beauty, my breast a grave for your travails. I'll love you the way fields love the spring, and live in you the way flowers live in the heat of the sun. I'll hum your name the way the valley echoes pealing bells reverberating above the village churches. I'll listen to the conversation of your soul the way the shore listens to the tales of the waves. I'll remember, Salma, the way a homesick expatriate remembers his beloved homeland, the starving beggar remembers a spread of luscious food, the de-

posed king remembers the days of his grandeur and luster, and the grief-stricken hostage recalls the hours of his liberty. I'll think about you the way a tiller thinks about his bushels of corn and the cereals on his threshing floor, the way the good shepherd thinks about green meadows and sweet springs."

While I was speaking, Salma was gazing into the depths of the night and sighing from time to time, her pulse speeding and undulating like waves of the sea, with their crests and troughs. Then she said, "To-morrow, reality will be a phantom and wakefulness will itself be no more than a dream. Can one pos-sessed by longing be contented with the embrace of an apparition, or the thirst of the parched be quenched by dream-springs?"

"Tomorrow," I said, "fate will convey you to the bosom of a family filled with repose and tranquillity, but it will drag me into the arena of the world, of struggle and discord. You to the house of a man who will rejoice in your beauty and in the purity of your soul, and I to the cavern of days that will torment me with their sorrows and terrify me with their specters. You to life, and I to battle. You to intimacy and friend-ship, and I to loneliness and solitude. But I will raise up in the valley of the shadow of death an idol to love, and I will worship it. I will take love as my entertainer, listening to its songs, drinking its wine, wearing its robes. At dawn, love will awaken me from my slumber and lead me to the distant, open country. At noon it will conduct me to the shade of trees, that I might lie down with the sparrows who are protected from the heat of the sun. In the evening it will cause me to stand before the sunset and will fill my ears with the melodies of nature's farewell to the light. It will show me the apparitions of stillness soaring in the void. At night it will embrace me and I will sleep, dreaming of celestial worlds where the spirits of lovers and poets reside.

In the spring I will walk beside love, and we will sing among the hills and lowlands, following the traces of life's footsteps marked by the violets and daisies, drinking the remnants of rainwater from flagons of narcissus and iris. In the summer, love and I will rest our heads on beds of straw, spreading out grasses, taking the sky as our blanket, and staying up late with the moon and the stars. In the autumn I will go with love to the vineyards and sit near the wine presses, gazing at the trees as they disrobe, contemplating the flocks of birds departing for the plains. In the winter I will sit with love near the glowing hearth, reciting tales of past centuries and repeating the chronicles of nations and peoples. In the days of youth love will be my mentor; in middle age it will be my support; and in old age it will be my companion. Love will stay with me, Salma, till the end of my life, until death comes, until God's grasp unites me with you."

The words rose urgently from the depths of my soul, as though they were flames of fire that grew and flew in all directions, then dissipated and waned in the corners of that garden. Salma was listening, tears flowing from her eyes as though her eyelids were lips that replied with tears to my words.

Those on whom love has never bestowed wings cannot soar beyond the clouds to see that enchanted realm wherein my spirit encircled that of Salma at that moment, so tragic in its joys and so blissful in its agonies. Those whom love has not chosen as disciples cannot hear love speak. This story was not written for them. Even if they fathomed the meaning of these faint pages, they could not perceive the ghosts and apparitions hovering between its lines, upon whom the ink bestows no robes and who do not take the written page for their dwelling place. Yet what human being has not sipped wine from one of its vessels? What soul has not stood awestruck in that illumined temple embellished with seeds of the heart and roofed over with mysteries, dreams, and feelings? On the petals of which flower has morning not poured a droplet of dew? What stream loses its way and does not flow into the sea?

At that point, Salma raised her head toward the spangled sky, stretching forth her hand. Her eyes widened, her lips trembled, and there appeared on her wan face all the protests, despair, and pain that lived within the soul of that wronged woman. Then she wailed, "What has woman done, my Lord, to merit your wrath? What sin did she commit, that your displeasure should follow her to the end of time? Did she perpetrate an infinitely loathsome crime, such that you have meted out to her a never-ending punishment? You are almighty, Lord, and she is frail, so why do you annihilate her with suffering? You are Most Great and she crawls before your throne, so why do you crush her beneath your feet? You are a raging tempest and she is like dust before your face, so why do you cast her down upon the snow? You are All-Conquering, and she is a wretch, so why do you make war on her? You are All-Seeing and All-Wise, and she is blind and lost, so why do you obliterate her?

You create her with love, how can you destroy her with love? With your right hand you lift her up unto you, and with your left you thrust her into the abyss, while she remains ignorant, not knowing why you raise her up or why you thrust her away. Into her mouth you blow the breath of life and in her heart you sow the seeds of death. On the paths of happiness, you send her forth without a steed; then you dispatch misery as a knight to hunt her down. From her throat you send forth songs of joy, then you seal her lips with grief and bind her tongue with sorrow. With your invisible fingers, you cause her agonies to speak of delights, and with your manifest fingers you etch halos of heartache around her pleasures. In her bed you conceal repose and peace, and beside her bed you draw terrors and travails. By your will you bring to life her desires, and from her desires you generate her faults and missteps. By your volition you show her the beauty of your creatures, then you transform her love for beauty into a fatal hunger. By your law you marry her spirit to a comely body, and by your decree you appoint her body lord over weakness and abasement.

"You pour out life for her into the cup of death, and death into the cup of life. You purify her by her tears, and by her tears you sap her of energy. You fill her insides with the bread of the male, then fill the palm of the man with grains from her breast.

"You, you, my Lord, opened my eyes by means of love, and by means of love you blinded me. You kissed me with your lips and your mighty hand buffeted me. You cast into my heart white rose seeds, then caused thorns to grow up all around that flower. You assured my present through the spirit of a young man whom I love, and by the body of a man whom I do not know. You have set a limit to my days, which helps to be strong in this mortal combat and aids me in remaining faithful and pure unto death. Thy will be done, my Lord. But your name is blessed until the end."

Salma fell silent, but her features continued to

speak. Her head bowed, her arms fell to her sides, and her frame drooped as though the vital force had abandoned her. To my eyes, she looked like a branch shattered by a storm and cast down on lowlands to wither and be scattered beneath the feet of time. I took her icy fingers in my fevered hand and kissed her fingertips with my eyelids and then my lips. When I tried to console her with words, I realized that I was more in need of consoling and sympathy than she. So I remained silent, bewildered, contemplating and deeply feeling the way the passing moments played with my emotions. I listened to the moaning of my heart within me, fearful of my soul for the sake of my soul.

Neither of us uttered a single word during what remained of that night, for the ardor of love when it becomes great turns to speechlessness. We remained quiet, frozen like two marble columns buried in the earth by an earthquake. Neither of us wanted to hear the other speak, for the fibers of our hearts had been enfeebled so that even a sigh, much less talking, was enough to rupture them.

Midnight arrived, and our dread of the silence grew. The moon rose, no longer full, from behind Mt. Sannin. Among the stars, it resembled the pasty face of a corpse, drowning amid the black pillows and faint candles surrounding it. Lebanon itself looked like an old man, his back bent by the years, his frame

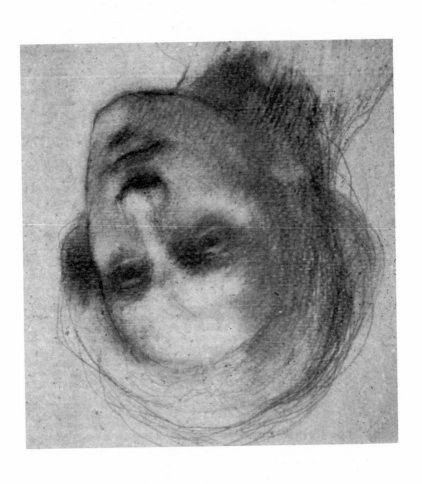

bowed by tribulations, his eyes abandoned by sleep—so that he kept the gloom company, awaiting the dawn the way an ousted king sits on the ashes of his throne among the ruins of his castle. The mountains, trees, and rivers modify their form and appearance when the situation and the times alter, just as the expressions on a human face change when thoughts and emotions do. The white poplar—which stands during the day like a lovely bride, the breeze playing with the lace of her dress—appears at night to be a pillar of smoke that ascends toward nothingness. The great boulder that sits at noon like a powerful tyrant mocking the vicissitudes of time looks at night like a wretched pauper sleeping on the ground, with the sky for a blanket. The stream that we see in the morning, glinting like molten silver, and which we hear singing the melodies of eternity, strikes our imaginations at night as a gully filled with tears that gush from the side of the valley, which we hear wailing and lamenting like a mother bereaved of her child. The Lebanon that had loomed a week before replete with glory and splendor when the moon was full and the soul well-contented, appeared in that night as depleted, miserable, and desolate before a feeble, partial moon that wandered confused in the high heavens and before a fluttering, ailing heart within its breast.

We stood to say good-bye, and love and despair stood between us like two terrifying specters, the one spreading its wings above our heads and the other seizing our necks in its talons. The one wept in empathy, the other laughed with scorn. When I took Salma's hand and put it to my lips to receive her blessing, she drew near me and kissed my hair on the part. Then she turned back and threw herself on the wooden bench, closing her eyes and whispering slowly, "Have mercy, Lord, and lend strength to all broken wings."

I parted from Salma and left the garden, feeling as though a heavy veil had descended over my senses, the way fog engulfs the surface of a lake. As I walked, the forms of the trees standing on either side of the road began to move before me, as though they were ghosts ascended from fissures in the earth to petrify me, and the soft rays of moonlight darted among the branches as though they were arrows of a moment, feathered by genie-spirits and soaring through the void toward my breast. A profound silence settled over me, like the heavy black hands of darkness on my body.

Everything in existence, every meaning in life, every mystery in the soul had turned ugly, horrifying, and bewildering. The spiritual light that had shown me the beauty of the world and the delights of existing things had metamorphosed into a fire that seared my heart with flames and shrouded it with smoke. The melody that had embraced the voices of all created beings and rendered them a celestial hymn had dissolved at that hour into a cacophony more bone-chilling than the roar of a lion, issuing from depths lower even than hell.

I arrived at my room and threw myself on my bed, like a bird hit by a hunter that falls into an enclosure with an arrow through its heart. My mind alternated between a frightening wakefulness and a troubled sleep, while my spirit repeated in both states Salma's words: "Have mercy, Lord, and lend strength to all broken wings."

BEFORE THE THRONE OF DEATH

Weddings these days have become little more than commercial enterprises, making one laugh and weep, of which young men and fathers of girls take charge. The young men win in most countries, and the fathers nearly always lose. As for the girls, who are shipped about like commodities from one house to another, their delights fade; like pieces of old furniture their fate is to be shunted into the corners of the house, where gloom and slow decline await them.

The civilization of the present day has increased the perceptiveness of women a bit, but it has multiplied their pain by making the aspirations of men theirs, as well. Women of yesterday were happy in serving, whereas today they are miserable mistresses. Yesterday they were blind, walking in the light of the day; but having become sighted, they now walk in the darkness of the night. They were lovely in their ignorance, virtuous in their simplicity, powerful in their weakness; they have become plain in their versatility, superficial in their perceptions, alienated from the heart by their knowledge. Will a day come that unites in women beauty and knowledge, versatility and virtue, delicacy of body and strength of soul? I am among those who maintain that spiritual advancement is the wont of humankind, and progress toward perfection is a gradual but effective law. If women have achieved progress on some fronts but not on others, it is because the narrow passes that allow us to reach the mountain top are not devoid of bandits' hideouts and wolf-infested caverns. On this mountain that resembles the oblivion you experience just before you wake up, on this mountain that grasps in its hands the earth of past centuries and the seeds of future generations, on this mountain of strange desires and hopes no city lacks a woman who symbolizes by her existence the daughter of the future. Salma Karama served in Beirut as a symbol of the coming Eastern woman. But she, like the many who lived before her time, was given up as a sacrifice to the present. Like a flower carried away by the river's current, she was coerced into life's march toward hardship.

Mansur Bey Ghalib married Salma, and they lived together in a splendid mansion standing near the seashore in Ras Beirut, where the cream of society and the very wealthy make their homes. Faris Karama remained alone in that isolated house among gardens and orchards, the way a shepherd is isolated among his sheep. The days of the nuptials passed, the nights of celebration were over, and the month elapsed that people call a honeymoon, which leaves in its wake months of bitterness and bile, the way the glories of war leave the skulls of the dead on distant fields. The empty show of Eastern weddings lifts up the souls of young men and women, like the flight of the eagle beyond the clouds. Then it casts them down like a millstone plummeting to the depths of the open sea— or, rather, the letdown is like footsteps on a seashore that last only till the waves efface them.

The spring departed, summer followed, and then autumn arrived, and my love for Salma evolved from the ardor that a young man in the morning of his life feels for a beautiful woman to the sort of mute adoration an orphan feels toward the spirit of a mother who dwells in eternity. The adolescence that had possessed me completely was transformed into a blind grief that sees only itself, and the passion that had provoked tears in my eyes became an ardent love that

distilled droplets of blood from my heart. The gasp-
ing sighs that had filled my lungs became deep prayers
performed by my spirit in stillness beneath the heavens, asking happiness for Salma, joy for her husband,
and reassurance for her father. But in vain did I sym-
pathize, implore, and pray, because Salma's misery
was a sickness in the soul that can be healed only by
death. As for her husband, he was one of those men
who acquire without exertion everything that makes
life pleasant, but still are not satisfied; rather, they
are always greedy for what they do not have. That is
the way they remain, tortured by their ambitions till
the end of their days. In vain I hoped for peace of
mind for Faris Karama, because no sooner his son-
in-law accepted the hand of Salma and acquired her
considerable wealth than he forgot Faris Karama and
abandoned him. Indeed, Mansur Bey began seeking
the old man's death so as to lay hands on the rest of
his riches.

Mansur Bey was like his uncle, the archbishop;
the nephew's character was the same, and his soul
was a small image of the other's. There was no differ-
ence between them except in the way that vainglory
differs from caution. Archbishop Ghalib achieved his
designs while veiled in his violet raiments and satisfied his cravings while seeking refuge in the golden
crucifix hanging on his breast. As for his nephew, he
did all that openly and forcibly. The archbishop went

to the cathedral in the morning and spent what was left of the day snatching money from widows, orphans, and the simplehearted. As for Mansur Bey, he spent the entire day following his pleasures and satisfying his appetites in dark alleys where the air is fermented by the breaths of depravity.

The archbishop stood on Sundays before the altar and preached to the believers, giving them advice he did not take himself; and he passed the days of the week immersed in the country's politics. His nephew, on the other hand, spent every day trading on the influence of his uncle among those who were seeking official positions or climbing the social ladder. The archbishop was a burglar concealed by the blanket of night; Mansur Bey was a confidence man walking boldly in the light of day.

Thus are people annihilated between burglars and confidence men, just as a flock meets its death between the claws of wolves and the knives of butchers. Thus do Eastern peoples submit to those with crooked souls and corrupt morals, retreating backward, then falling into the abyss, while time passes and grinds them with its feet the way iron hammers smash the vases of the proud.

What makes me now worry these pages with words about miserable, wretched nations, I wonder, when I had dedicated them to recording the tale of a heartbroken woman and to depicting the ghosts haunting a heart in pain that had remained untouched by love's joys when it slapped him in the face with its sorrows? Why do tears run from my eyes at the mention of obscure, oppressed peoples, when I have stopped my tears at the memory of a powerless woman who had barely embraced life when death took her in its arms? But is not a frail woman a symbol for an exploited nation? Is not a woman torn painfully between the desires of her soul and the bonds of her body like a persecuted country caught between its rulers and its priests? Are not the invisible tempests that hurl a beautiful young woman into the gloom of a grave like the severe storms that bury the lives of people under silt? A woman is to a nation as a ray is to a lamp; can the rays of the lamp be faint if its oil has not run low?

The days of fall passed and the winds disgraced the trees by toying with their yellowed leaves, the way whirlpools play with ocean foam. Winter came, weeping and sobbing, while I was in Beirut without a companion save my dreams, which lifted up my soul sometimes, taking it all the way to the stars, and descended with my heart at others, taking it to the interior of the earth.

The disconsolate soul finds repose in withdrawal and solitude, fleeing people the way a wounded gazelle distances itself from the herd and conceals itself until it recovers or dies.

One day I heard that Faris Karama had fallen ill, so I gave up my hermit-like existence and went to cheer him up. I followed an isolated path between olive trees, their lead-gray leaves glistening with rain-drops, and avoided the public thoroughfare where the din of traffic disturbed the tranquillity of the heavens.

I reached the old man's house and entered, finding him sprawled across his bed, his body gaunt, his face haggard, his color yellowish. His eyes had sunk beneath his brows and looked like two deep, jet caverns wherein roamed the specters of sickness and pain. His face which had only yesterday been the epitome of good humor and cheerfulness, had contracted, darkened, and become like an ashen, wrinkled page upon which infirmity had inscribed eerie, obscure lines. The hands that had been enveloped in grace and gentleness had wasted away until the bones were visible beneath the skin, like exposed twigs shaking in a squall.

When I approached him and asked how he was, he turned his pinched face toward me, and on his twitching lips there appeared the shadow of a melancholy smile. In an insubstantial, fading voice that you might imagine was issuing from behind the walls, he said, "Go, my son, go to that room. Wipe Salma's tears away and quiet her anxiety. Then come back with her and sit on the side of my bed."

I entered the facing room and found Salma draped over a chair, her head buried in her arms, her face drowned in cushions, choking back her sobs lest her father hear her weeping. I came toward her slowly, pronouncing her name in a voice closer to a sigh than to a whisper. She moved, unsettled, like a sleeper disturbed by nightmares. Then she straightened up in her chair and looked at me with a fixed, unwavering gaze, as though she were seeing a phantasm in the world of visions and did not believe I was really in that place.

After a profound silence, which by its mystical influence returned us to those times wherein we had become drunk on the wine of the gods, Salma brushed at her tears with her fingertips and said in distress, "Do you see how the times have changed? Have you seen how time misled us so that we hurried to these horrifying caves? In this place, spring brought us together in the grasp of love, and in this place now winter has brought us together before the throne of death. How glorious that day was, and how black is this night."

She said these words, repressing her sobs toward the end. Then she put her face in her hands, as though the memory of the past had become incarnate and stood before her, and she did not want to see it. I put my hands on her hair and said, "Come on, Salma. Let's stand like towers before the storm. Let's stand like an army before the enemy, meeting their sword blades with our breasts and not with our backs. If we are felled, we'll die as martyrs, but if we prevail, we'll live as heroes. For the soul to experience torment because of its perseverance in the face of trials and difficulties is more noble than for it to retreat to a place of safety and calm. The moth that continues to flutter about the lamp until it burns up is more exalted than the mole that lives in comfort and security in its dark tunnel. The seed that cannot bear the cold of winter and the turbulence of the elements is not strong enough to break through the earth and will never delight in the beauty of April.

"Come on, Salma, let's set out with firm feet on this rugged path, keeping our eyes on the sun, lest we see the skulls scattered among the rocks and the vipers slithering among the thornbushes. If fear stops us in the middle of the road, the phantoms of night will treat us to loud ridicule and derision; if we reach the summit of the mountain by our courage, the spirits of the heavens will sing with us the victory anthem. Don't be so hard on yourself, Salma. Dry your tears and put away that forlorn expression. Get up, and let's go sit beside your father's bed, since he draws life from your life and will be healed by your smile."

She looked at me with a gaze full of kindness, compassion, and affection, then said, "You're asking me to be patient and persevering when your eyes are epitomes of despair and hopelessness? Does a starving pauper give his bread to a pauper who is starving? Or does a sick person prescribe a remedy to an ill friend when he himself is in greater need of it?"

She stood up and, shaking her head, led me into her father's room. We sat next to the ailing old man's bed, and Salma feigned a smile and peace of mind, while he affected repose and strength. But both of them felt the other's agony, knowing the other's weakness and listening to the groans of the other's heart. They were like two equal forces that canceled one another out and left only stillness. A seriously ill father melts, careworn, at his daughter's misery. A loving daughter wastes away, aching at her father's illness. A departing soul and a despondent soul embrace before love and death; I stood between them, burdened by what was inside me and suffering at what was within them. Three whom the hand of destiny had gathered together, then squeezed in its grasp until it crushed them. An old man representing an ancient house razed by a hurricane; a young woman like a lily, mown down by the blade of a scythe; a young man like a frail sapling, bent under the weight of the snow—all of us like playthings in the hands of fate.

The old man moved then, under the covers, and reached out his emaciated hand toward Salma. In a voice imbued with all the tenderness and kindness that lives in a father's heart and all the sickness and pain that subsists in the breast of the ill, he said, "Put your hand in mine, Salma."

She stretched out her hand, thrusting it between his fingers. He clasped it with kindness, then added, "I've had my fill of years, child. I've lived long, savored the fruits produced by each season, and enjoyed everything yielded by days and nights. I slept late as a boy, embraced love as a young man, and made a fortune in my middle age; and in every one of those stages of my life, I was happy and exhilarated. I lost your mother, Salma, before you turned three, but she left you for me as an inestimable treasure. You grew up so fast, like a moon going through its phases, and your mother's features were reflected in your face the way starlight is reflected in a placid pool of water. Her traits and her character appeared in your actions and words, as gold jewelry glitters behind a diaphanous veil. I consoled myself with you, child, because you were like her, beautiful and wise. But now I have grown old. The old find rest within the soft wings of death. Take comfort, child, that I lived to see you a grown woman and rejoice, because through you I will live on after my death. For me to go now is no different from my going tomorrow or the next day, for our days are like autumn leaves that fall and disperse before the face of the sun. Should the hours hurry me off to eternity, it is because they know my spirit yearns to meet with your mother."

He spoke the final words in a melody imbued with the sweetness of hope and longing. On his downcast face appeared rays like the light that twinkles in a child's eyes. He put his hand into the pillows surrounding his head and pulled from them a small, old photograph framed in gold, its edges softened by the touch of hands, its outlines faded by the kiss of lips. He said, without lifting his eyes from the picture, "Come close, Salma, my child. I want to show you an image of your mother. Come, look at her shadow on a piece of paper."

Salma drew near, wiping the tears from her eyes lest they keep her from seeing the faded picture. After she had stared at it a long while, as though it were a mirror reflecting her own attributes, appearance, and face, she brought it to her lips and kissed it impatiently, over and over again. Then she cried out, saying, "Mama! Oh, Mama!" She added nothing to this, but put the picture to her trembling lips as though attempting to instill it with life by her hot breath.

The sweetest thing human lips can say is the word "Mother," and the most beautiful of calls is "O Mother." It is a word both small and large, filled with hope and love and emotion, and all the delicacy and sweetness that exists in the human breast. A mother is everything in this life: She consoles in grief; she

gives hope in sorrow and power in weakness. She is a fountain of compassion, mercy, and forgiveness. Whoever loses a mother loses a breast to lean his head against, a hand to bless him, and an eye to watch over him.

Everything in nature symbolizes and speaks of motherhood. The sun is the mother of this earth, which it nurses with its warmth and hugs with its light, and which it never leaves in the evening without first putting it to sleep with the lullaby of ocean waves, the warbling of birds, and the purling of brooks. This earth is a mother to the trees and flowers, to which it gives birth and which it nurses and then weans. Then the trees and flowers, in their turn, become affectionate mothers to luscious fruits and living seeds. The mother of all things in existence is the Universal Spirit, which is immortal and everlasting, and filled with beauty and love.

Salma Karama never knew her mother because she had died when Salma was a little girl, and she was so affected when she saw the picture of her mother that a gasp escaped her and she involuntarily called out, "Mother!" For the word "mother" is concealed in our hearts the way atoms are hidden in the heart of the world, and it is spoken by our lips in times of sorrow and joy, just as the heart of a flower gives off its perfume when the skies are clear and when it rains.

Salma stared at the picture of her mother, then kissed it with a sigh and clasped it to her heaving bosom. She moaned, sighing, and with every sigh she lost a portion of her strength. When the spirit drained out of her frail body, she fell to her knees beside her father's bed. He put his hands on her head, saying, "I showed you, my child, a likeness of your mother on a piece of paper. Now listen to me, as I relate to you her words."

Salma raised her head the way a hen on her nest does when she hears the rustling of the wings of sparrows between the bars. She looked at him, listening meekly, as though her spiritual essence had been transformed into staring eyes or listening ears.

Her father said, "You were a babe in arms when your mother lost her elderly father, and she grieved at the loss, but wept only stoically. As soon as she returned from his graveside, she sat next to me in this very room and took my hand in hers.

"She said, 'My father has died, Faris. But you remain with me, and that is my consolation. The heart, with its many emotions, is like a cedar with its different branches. When the cedar loses a strong branch, it feels pain, but it does not die. Instead, it transfers its vital energies to a nearby branch so that it can grow, filling with its lush twigs the place of the broken-off branch.'

"That's what your mother said, Salma, when her father died. That is what you must say when death takes my body to the peace of the grave and my spirit to the shadow of God."

Salma replied, distressed, "My mother lost her father, but you remained with her. Who will remain with me when I lose you, father? Her father died when she was in the shadow of a loving, virtuous, and trustworthy husband; her father died when she had a baby girl to bury her head in her breasts and to throw her little arms around her neck. Who will remain with me if I lose you, father? You are my father and mother, the companion of my youth and mentor of my adolescence. With whom could I replace you if you go?"

She said this, then turned her tearful eyes toward me and grasped my lapel with her right hand. "I have only this friend, father, and only he remains to me when you leave me. Can I be consoled by him, when he is tortured, just as I am? Can the brokenhearted seek solace from the heartbroken? A grief-stricken woman takes no comfort from the grief of her neighbor, just as a dove cannot fly with broken wings. He is a soul mate, but I have piled up my worries on his shoulders until his back is bent and his eyes are exhausted by my tears and can see only gloom. He is a brother whom I love and who loves me, but he, like all brothers, shares in the calamity and cannot lighten it; he joins in the weeping but makes the tears more bitter and adds to the flames consuming the heart."

As I listened to Salma speaking, my emotions became more intense, and my heart was constricted, till I felt as though my ribs would explode and riddle me with holes.

As for the old man, he gazed at her as his wasted body sank slowly into the cushions and pillows, and his enervated soul wavered like the flame of a lamp before the wind. Then he stretched out his arms and said quietly, "Let me go in peace, my child. My eyes have glimpsed what lies beyond the mists, and I will never again turn them toward these caverns. Let me fly, for I have smashed the bars of this cage with my wings. Your mother has called me, Salma, so don't stop me. . . . Look, a pleasant wind has come up and the mists have dissipated from the surface of the sea. The ship has raised its sails and made ready to depart, so don't stop me, don't block the helm. Let my body lie down with the others already stretched out, and let my spirit awaken, because the morn has broken and patience is exhausted. . . . Kiss my spirit with yours. Give me the kiss of hope, and don't spill a drop of bitter grief on my body, lest the grasses and flowers be prevented from imbibing my elements. Don't pour tears of misery on my hand, for they will grow into thorns above my grave. Don't inscribe on my brow a single line with the sighs of mourning, for the dawn breeze will pass by and read it, and will not carry the dust of my bones to verdant meadows. . . . I loved you in life, my child, and I will love you in death. My spirit will stay near to protect and safeguard you."

The old man turned to me, his eyelids drooping somewhat, so that I could no longer see anything but two gray lines where his eyes were. He said, his words softened by the stillness of cessation, "As for you, my son, be a brother to Salma the way your father was to me. Be close by during her hours of tribulation. Be a friend to her to the end, and do not leave her to grieve, for mourning the dead is an error committed during past centuries. Rather, recite for her ears sayings of joy and sing for her hymns of life so that she will forget and become oblivious. . . . Tell your father to remember me. Ask him, and he will tell you about my early days, when youth used to carry us up to the clouds. Tell him that I loved him in the person of his son at the last moment of my life."

He fell silent while the wraiths of his words crawled along the walls of the room. Then he looked at me and at Salma all at once and said in a whisper, "Don't call a doctor, so that he might prolong my time in prison with his nostrums. The days of my servitude have passed and my spirit has requested the freedom of the void. Don't call a priest to my bedside, because his rites will not absolve me of my sins if I am a transgressor, nor hasten my journey to heaven if I am innocent. Human wills cannot alter the will of God, just as astronomers cannot change the paths of the stars. When I am dead, let the doctors and priests do as they will, for the depths of the sea call to the depths of the sea; but as for the ship, it goes on sailing until it reaches the shore."

When midnight struck on that frightful night, Faris Karama opened his eyes, which were sunk in the shadows of his death struggle. He opened them for the last time and turned them toward his daughter, who was kneeling by the side of his bed. He tried to speak but could not, for death had imbibed his voice. Then the words issued from his lips in a deep gasp: "Look, the night is over. . . . Morning is coming . . . Salma . . . Oh, Salma."

His head drooped, his face went pale, his lips smiled, and he surrendered up his spirit.

Salma stretched out her hand and touched her father's hand, finding it cold as snow. She lifted her head and looked at him, seeing his face covered by the veil of death. The life froze in her body, her tears dried in their tracks, and she stayed stock still. She did not cry out or wail, but only stared at him with a fixed gaze, like that of a statue. Her limbs went limp, like the pleats in a dress that has gotten wet, and she collapsed in a heap, her brow touching the floor. She said quietly, "Have mercy, O Lord, and strengthen all broken wings."

Faris Karama died, his spirit embraced eternity, and his body returned to the earth. Mansur Bey got hold of all his wealth, and his daughter remained a prisoner of her misery, seeing life as a terrifying tragedy played out by horrors before her eyes.

As for me, I was lost between my dreams and my apprehensions, torn by the days and nights as if by falcons and eagles. How I tried to lose myself in the pages of books, that I might commune with the shades of those whom time had swallowed up! How I tried to forget my present, so as to return, by reading, to the vistas of past centuries. But none of it was any use—I was like a man trying to put out a fire with oil. I could see nothing in the pageant of the centuries save black phantasms, and I heard no songs of the various peoples save dirges and laments. The Book of Job was more beautiful in my eyes than the Psalms of David, and the Lamentations of Jeremiah were more beloved than the Song of Solomon. I was more impressed by the fall of the Barmakid viziers than by the grandeur of the Abbasid empire that they served; the *Ode of Ibn Zurayq* affected me more deeply than

Khayyam's *Rubáiyát*; and Shakespeare's *Hamlet* was closer to my heart than anything else written by Western authors.

Thus does despair weaken our vision, so that we see nothing but our own bone-chilling ghosts; thus does despondency stop up our ears, so that we hear only the agitated pounding of our own hearts.

BETWEEN
ASTARTE AND CHRIST

Among the gardens and hillocks that connect the outskirts of Beirut with the foothills of Lebanon, there
stands an ancient, diminutive place of worship carved
into the heart of a white boulder among olive, almond,
and willow trees. Although this temple lay no more
than half a mile from the carriage route, few among the
lovers of antiquities and ancient ruins knew of it. It
was like many important things in Syria, hidden behind the veils of neglect; and it was as though neglect
had kept it hidden from the eyes of archaeologists, so
as to make it a sanctuary for the souls of the weary and
a pilgrimage site for lonely lovers.

Those who entered that eerie tabernacle saw on its east wall a frieze of Phoenician appearance; and of the phrases carved into the stone, the fingers of time had erased some lines and the seasons had highlighted others colorfully. It depicted Astarte, the goddess of love and beauty, seated on an august throne, surrounded by seven nude virgins standing in various poses. The first carries a torch, the second a lute, the third the censer, the fourth a wine jar, the fifth a rose stem, the sixth a crown of laurel, and the seventh a bow and arrow. All of them are gazing at Astarte with expressions of submission and obedience on their faces.

On the second wall is another picture, from a more recent age and more distinct, showing Jesus of Nazareth crucified; on one side of him is his mourning mother and Mary Magdalene, with two other sobbing women. This scene, with its Byzantine style and trademarks, gives evidence of having been carved in the fifth or sixth Christian century.

On the west wall are two circular apertures through which the rays of the sun entered in late afternoon, spilling onto the two friezes and making them appear as though they had been laminated with golden water.

In the center of the temple stands a square block of marble. On its surface were marks and inscriptions that appeared ancient, some of them hidden beneath petrified layers of blood, which proved that the most ancient worshippers there had slaughtered their sacrifices on the stone, then poured over them offerings of wine, perfume, and oil.

There was nothing else in this small house of worship save a profound stillness that embraced the soul and a magical awe that betrayed through its reverberations the secrets of the gods and that spoke without utterance of the origins of bygone generations and the transition of peoples from one state to another, from one religion to another. Such images incline the poet to seek a world far distant from this one, and convince the philosopher that human beings are religious creatures who sense what they do not see and conceive what they do not perceive. So humans draw up symbols to express these feelings and to point by their meanings toward the mysteries of the soul and to incarnate their imaginings in word, song, and image. These manifest by their outward forms humanity's holiest yearnings in life and their most beautiful goals after death.

In that unknown temple I used to meet Salma Karama once a month, and we would spend long hours scrutinizing the strange images and thinking about the Son of the Generations crucified on Golgotha. We pictured in our imaginations the ghosts of the Phoenician young men and women who lived

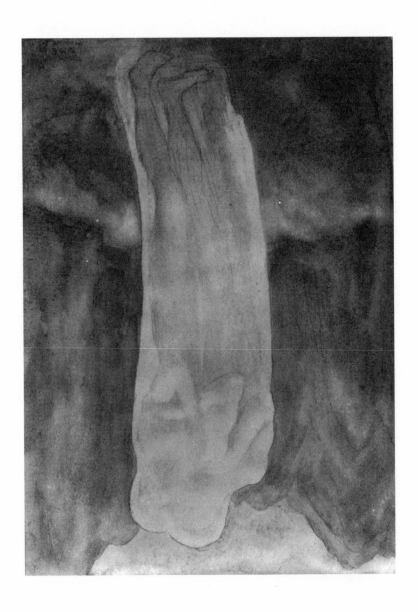

and loved and worshipped beauty in the person of Astarte, who burned incense before her idols and offered up perfumes on her altar. Then the earth enfolded them and nothing remained of them save a name bandied about by the days before the face of eternity.

How difficult it is for me now to record in words the memory of those hours that united me with Salma—those sublime hours suffused with pleasure and pain, bliss and sadness, hope and despair, with everything that renders a human being human and life an everlasting riddle. But how difficult it is for me to mention it and not to delineate in feeble words an image of her that might endure as an ideal to the children of love and grief.

We used to retire to that ancient temple and sit in its threshold, leaning against its walls, as we returned to the echoes of our past, probed the origins of our present situation, and grew fearful for our future. Then we gradually proceeded to reveal what was in our inmost souls, complaining each in turn of our lovesickness, the fire consuming our hearts, and the anxiety and sorrow we were suffering. We each gave the other courage by spreading before us the glad imaginings and pleasant dreams that jingle in hope's pockets. Our alarm would subside, our tears would dry, our expressions would show relief, and we would smile, ignoring everything but love and its joys, turning away from all else save the soul and its cravings. Then we would embrace and melt in sensual desire and crazed love. Salma would kiss my hair with purity and affection, filling my heart with light. I would kiss her white fingertips, and she would close her eyes and turn her ivory neck, her cheeks tinged with a pink like the first rays that dawn casts on hillcrests. We would then fall silent, gazing for a long while toward the distant horizon and the tangerine clouds of sunset.

Our meetings were not confined to exchanges of emotion and complaints; rather, we would unwittingly stray into generalities, exchanging views and thoughts about the affairs of this strange world, discussing the intent of the books we were reading, making observations on their virtues and vices and the imagery and social principles they contained. Salma spoke of the place of women in human society, the influence of past generations on society's morals and inclinations, and the relationship between spouses in this day, as well as the diseases and corruption that afflicted it.

I remember that one time she said, "Writers and poets try to perceive the reality of woman, but at present they have not understood the secrets of her heart and the mysteries concealed in her breast, because they look at her from behind the veil of lust, seeing nothing but her figure; or they put her under the magnifying glass of misogyny and find nothing in her but weakness and submission."

On another occasion she said to me, as she pointed at the two pictures carved into the walls of the temple, "On the heart of this stone generations have engraved two pictures that demonstrate the essence of woman's desires and make clear the obscurities of her soul, which vacillates between love and sorrow, affection and sacrifice—between Astarte sitting on her throne and Mary standing before the Cross. A man buys glory, grandeur and fame, but it is woman who pays the price."

No one knew of our secret assignations save God and the flocks of sparrows flying among those gardens. Salma would come in her carriage to the place called the Pasha's Garden, then would walk unhurriedly along the isolated pathways until she reached the little house of worship. She would enter therein, leaning on her parasol. Her face gleamed with security and composure. She would find me eagerly awaiting her, with all the hunger and thirst of passionate yearning.

We never in any way feared being observed, nor did we feel the slightest prick of conscience. When the soul has been purified by fire and washed by tears, it rises above what the people call shame and disgrace. It liberates itself from slavery to the laws and norms that custom has legislated for the emotions of the human heart, and stands, head held high, before the thrones of the gods.

Human society has surrendered for seventy centuries to corrupt laws and is no longer able to perceive the true meaning of the sublime, primary, and eternal codes of behavior. Human vision has become accustomed to looking at the light of feeble candles and can no longer stare at the light of the sun. Each generation has inherited the psychological diseases and maladies of the others, and so these have become universal. They have become attributes inseparable from humanity, so that people no longer look upon them as diseases but consider them natural and noble qualities revealed by God to Adam. And when a person appears among them who lacks these traits, they see that individual as flawed and deprived of spiritual perfections.

As for those who will find fault with Salma Karama, attempting to sully her name because she used to leave her lawful husband's house to rendezvous with another man, they are sick and weak. They reckon the upright as criminals and those with self-respect as rebels. They are like insects that creep in the darkness and fear to emerge into the light of day lest the feet of passersby stomp on them.

A wrongfully jailed man who can raze the walls of his prison but declines to do so is a coward. Salma Karama was unjustly imprisoned and could not

achieve her release. Should she be condemned because she looked out through the window of the
prison toward green fields and open spaces? Do people
consider her a traitor because she used to come from
the house of Mansur Bey Ghalib to sit beside me between holy Astarte and the crucified Conqueror? Let
the people say what they will, Salma traversed the
swamps in which their own spirits drown and attained
that world where the howling of wolves and the hiss
of vipers cannot reach. Let the people say what they
want about me, for the soul that has seen the counte-
nance of death cannot be frightened by a thief's face,
and the soldier who has seen swords crisscrossed
above his head and streams of blood running at his
feet pays no attention to the stone tossed at him by
small boys in an alley.

THE SACRIFICE

One day toward the end of June, when the heat lay heavily along the coast and the people had fled to the mountain heights, I was walking as usual toward that temple, having determined to meet Salma Karama. I carried in my hand a small book of Andalusian verse that used to entrance me in those days and still does now.

I arrived at the temple late in the afternoon and sat watching the paths that wound among the lemon and willow trees. From time to time I glanced at the cover of my book, whispering in the ears of the ether those verses which seduce the heart with the grace of their composition and the resonance of their meters.

They call up memories of the glories of the kings, poets and knights who relinquished Grenada, Cordova, and Seville, leaving behind all their souls' hopes and desires in those castles, familiar places, and gardens. Then they vanished behind the veils of the eons, tears on their eyelashes and grief in their bellies.

After an hour I looked up, and there was Salma's slender form swaying to and fro through the dense coppices. She leaned on her parasol as she approached me, as though weighed down with all the worries and burdens of the world. When she reached the door of the temple and sat next to me, I gazed into her large eyes and read in them strange new mysteries and meanings that inspired caution and vigilance, but also provoked extreme curiosity.

Salma sensed what was running through my mind, and she did not wish to prolong the battle between my imaginings and my misgivings. She put her hand on my head and said, "Come close, lover. Let me enrich my soul through you. For the hour is approaching when we will be separated forever."

I cried out, "What do you mean, Salma? What power could part us for eternity?"

She answered, "The blind power that separated us yesterday will do so tomorrow. The mute power that takes human laws as its spokesman has used the slaves of life to erect an impenetrable barrier between you and me. The power that created demons and made them guardians over human souls has decreed that I not issue from that house built of skulls and bones."

"Did your husband find out about our meetings? Are you afraid of his anger and vengeance?"

"My husband pays no attention to me and hasn't the slightest notion of how I spend my time. He's too busy with those poverty-stricken girls whose neediness drives them to the slave markets, so that they perfume themselves and make themselves up in order to sell their bodies for bread kneaded with blood and tears."

"Then what stops you from coming to this temple and sitting with me, awed by God and by phantoms of the past? Have you grown tired of gazing into the inner recesses of my soul, so that your spirit begs you to bid me farewell?"

She replied, a tear perched on her eyelid, "No, darling. My spirit has not asked me to leave you, because you are its shore. My eyes are not tired of looking at you because you are their light. But if destiny has ordained that I tread the steep paths of life weighed down with chains and manacles, can I desire to have you suffer the same fate?"

"Tell me everything, and don't leave out a single piece of this puzzle."

"I can't say everything, since lips paralyzed by pain cannot speak. All I can say to you is that I fear that you might fall into the snare of the ones who have tied me up and made me a captive."

"What do you mean? Who are these people who make you afraid for me?"

She hid her face in her hands and sighed with anguish. "The archbishop, Paul Ghalib, has found out that once a month I escape from the grave he put me in."

"Does the archbishop know that you meet me here?"

"If he knew that, you wouldn't be seeing me sitting here now, next to you. But doubts are fermenting in his mind and teasing his thoughts. He has sent spies to keep me under surveillance and given orders to the servants to monitor my movements. It's gotten to the point where I feel that even the house where I live and the street I walk on have eyes staring at me, fingers pointing at me, and ears that listen to the whispering of my thoughts."

She bowed her head in silence for a moment, and as tears cascaded down her cheeks, she added, "I am not afraid of the archbishop for myself. If you have already drowned, you are not afraid to get wet. But I am frightened for you. You are as free as a sunbeam—it would be a tragedy for you to fall into the same snare as I have, for him to get his talons into you and mangle you with his fangs. I'm not afraid of fate—it's already run out of arrows to pierce me. But

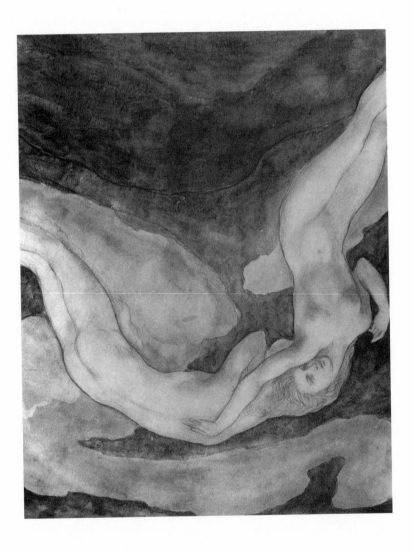

I am scared for you—you are too young to die of a snake bite on your way to the mountain peak, where all the joys and glory of your future are waiting for you."

"Only the deluded get through life without being bitten by snakes in the daytime and torn to shreds by wolves at night," I replied. "Listen to me well. Is there nothing ahead of us but being apart because we feared the pettiness and evil of other people? Are the roads to love, life, and freedom blocked before us? Do we have no choice but to bow before the will of death's slaves?"

Her voice was overcome by despair and sorrow. "There's nothing for us now but to bid each other farewell and go our separate ways."

I took her hand, my spirit rebelling within me, the fires of my young manhood raging. I cried out, "We've bowed for an eternity to the desires of the people. From the hour we met till now we've been led by the blind and we've knelt before their idols. Since I met you we've been like a couple of children's balls in the hands of Archbishop Paul Ghalib, and he's played with us however he's wanted, tossing us here and there. Are we going to keep on obeying him, staring out at the darkness of his soul until the grave gobbles us up and the earth swallows us? Has God bestowed on us the gift of life so that we can place it at death's feet? Has He given us liberty so that we can reduce it to the shadow of slavery? Anyone who puts out the fire of his soul with his own hands has betrayed the heavens, which lighted it. Whoever is patient in the face of oppression and refuses to rebel against tyranny is an ally of the wrong against the right, an accomplice to the murders of the innocent.

"I love you, Salma, and you love me. Love is a precious treasure that God places within great, sensitive souls. Are we going to toss our treasure into a pigsty so that the pigs can strew it about with their snouts and scatter it with their hooves? The world is a vast stage before us, filled with charm and wonder. Why should we live in this narrow tunnel that the archbishop and his helpers have dug? Life and freedom are before us and freedom's joy and happiness. Let us throw this heavy yoke off our shoulders, break the chains binding our legs, and go somewhere we can find peace and tranquillity. Get up, let's leave this little house of worship for God's most great temple. Come, we'll emigrate from this country, with all its slavery and stupidity, to some distant country where thieves' hands can't reach and demons won't breath down our necks. Come, let's hurry to the shore under cover of night and board a ship that will take us over the ocean, where we can live a new life of purity and mutual understanding. There no snake will be able to spray us with its venom and no beast will trample us underfoot. Don't hesitate. These seconds are more precious than the crowns of kings, more sublime than the thrones of angels. Get up! Let's follow the column of light, which will lead us from this barren desert to fields where flowers and wild herbs grow."

Salma shook her head, her eyes having made out some invisible thing in that temple. A sad smile stole across her lips, announcing the pain and stress in her soul. She said quietly, "No, darling. Heaven has put a cup of vinegar into my hand, and I drank it down all at once. There's nothing left in the cup but a few drops that I'll drink patiently, just to see the secrets and mysteries hidden at the bottom of the cup. As for that new, exalted life of love, repose, and peace of mind, I don't deserve it. I wouldn't be able to bear its joys and delights. A bird with two broken wings can crawl among the rocks, but it cannot fly, soaring into the sky. Weak eyes can stare at faint things, but they cannot bear to look at brilliant lights. So don't talk to me about happiness, because its mention pains me as though it were talk of misery. And don't imagine me in bliss, because its shadow scares me as much as wretchedness does. But look at me, so I can show you the sacred flame that heaven has ignited in the ashes of my breast. You know I love you the way a mother loves her only child. It's love that taught me to protect you, even from myself. Love, purified by fire, stops me now from following you to the ends of the earth and makes me kill my feelings and desires so that you can live free and remain untainted, protected from the blame and lying gossip of the people. Limited love demands possession of the beloved, but infinite love desires only its own essence. There is a love that comes between the wakefulness and heedlessness of youth, which contents itself with meeting someone and being with him, and which grows with kisses and hugs. But the love that is born in infinite breasts, which descends with the mysteries of night, cannot be content with less than eternity, and does not stand awestruck before anything but divinity.

"When I found out yesterday that Archbishop Paul Ghalib wants to forbid me from leaving the house of his nephew and to rob me of the one pleasure I've known since my wedding, I stood at my bedroom window and looked out on the sea, thinking about the wide countries, the spiritual freedom, and the personal liberty that lie beyond it. I imagined myself living with you, encompassed by your spirit, showered with your affection. But as soon as such daydreams—which illumine the breasts of downtrodden women and make them rebel against evil traditions so they can live in the shadow of truth and freedom—passed through my mind, I belittled myself and cursed myself for being weak, seeing our love as a paltry and feeble thing, unable to stand before the face of the sun. I cried like a king who has forfeited his kingdom or a rich man who has lost his treasures. But all the while I still saw your face through my tears, and noticed the way your eyes were staring at me. I remembered something you said to me once:

"'Let's go, Salma, and stand in front of our enemies and meet their sword blades with our breasts. If we are defeated, we'll die like martyrs. And if we prevail, we'll live like heroes. The torture a soul feels when being steadfast in the face of tribulation is more noble than its withdrawal into safety and security.'

"Those were your very words to me, darling, when the wings of death were fluttering around my father's bed. I remembered them yesterday, when the wings of despair were fluttering around my head. I took heart, and even in the depths of that prison I felt a sort of precious freedom, the sort that makes light of hardships and sorrows. I saw that our love rivaled the sea in its depth, the stars in their height, and space in its vastness. I came here today to you even as a new power has grown within my anguished soul, a power capable of sacrificing the great for what is greater yet, of sacrificing my happiness near you so that you can remain honorable in the eyes of the people and avoid their treachery and persecution. I was going to come to this place yesterday, but heavy chains bound my feet. But today I've come, infused with a determination that laughs at the weight of my manacles and finds the longest road a short walk. I was going to come like a fearful ghost knocking at the door, but today I have come like a live woman who feels the obligation to sacrifice, knows the value of pain, and wants to protect her beloved from idiots and from her own hungry soul. I used to sit before you like a trembling shadow, but today I've come to show you my reality before holy Astarte and Jesus crucified. I am a tree growing in the shadows, but today I have spread out my branches so they can sway in the light of day. I've come to say good-bye to you, darling. Let's make our parting as great and awesome a thing as our love. Let's make it like the fire that melts gold to render it more brilliant."

Salma left me no opportunity to speak or protest. Instead, she looked at me with flashing eyes, their rays dominating my consciousness. Her features veiled themselves behind an awe-inspiring splendor, and she looked like a queen who inspired silence and submission. Then she threw herself on my chest with absolute affection such as I had never seen from her before that moment. She draped her silky scarf around my neck and kissed my lips long, hard, and feverishly. Life awakened in my body, hidden mysteries were revealed in my soul, and the objective essence I call "I" rebelled against the whole world, seeking to obey implicitly the exalted Law that had taken Salma's breast for its temple and her soul for its altar.

When the sun set and its last rays were effaced from those gardens and orchards, Salma rose and stood in the middle of the temple, gazing for a long time at its walls and crannies, as though she wanted to illuminate its drawings and patterns with her eyes. She stepped forward and knelt humbly before the image of Jesus crucified, kissing his wounded feet again and again.

She whispered, "You chose your cross, Jesus of Nazareth, and forsook the joy and bliss of Astarte. I've placed a crown of thorns rather than of laurel on my head; I've bathed in my blood and tears instead of in perfumes. I drank vinegar from a cup designed for wine. Accept me, then, as one of your followers, who are strong in their weakness, and speed me toward Golgotha in the company of your chosen ones, who are content with their afflictions and blessed by the distress in their hearts.

She stood then and turned to me. "I'm going to return now joyfully to the gloomy cave where terrifying ghosts abide. Don't feel sorry for me, darling. Don't be sad for me. The soul that has once seen the shadow of God isn't afraid of demonic apparitions. An eye adorned even for a moment with the sight of the Concourse on High cannot be blinded by the calamities of this life."

Salma departed from that temple, wrapped in her

silky clothes. She left me lost and bewildered, full of thought. I was attracted to the plane of visions where the gods sit on their thrones, angels record the deeds of human beings, spirits chant the tragedies of life, and the brides of the imagination sing anthems of love and grief and immortality.

When I awakened from that stupor, the night having drowned the world in its pitch-black waves, I found myself wandering among those gardens, trying to recall the echo of every word Salma had pronounced, to recover in my soul her movements and stillnesses, the expressions on her face, and the touch of her hands. At length the reality of her farewell bore in on me, as did the pain of loneliness and the bitterness of yearning that would now be my lot. My thoughts froze, the fibers of my heart went limp, and I knew for the first time that a man, even though born free, remains in bondage to the cruel laws enacted by his fathers and grandfathers—and that destiny, of which we conceive as a sublime mystery, is simply today's surrender to tomorrow's eventualities and the submission of tomorrow to the desires of today. How many times have I thought, from that night to this day, of the precious laws that made Salma choose death over life. How often have I placed the nobility of sacrifice next to the happiness of rebellion to determine which is more glorious and more beautiful. But so far I can understand only one truth:

Sincerity renders all deeds good and noble. Salma Karama was sincerity personified and sound belief incarnate.

THE SAVED

Five years went by from the time of Salma's wedding, and she still had not been blessed with a child who might have established a spiritual relationship between her and her husband, whose precious smile might have united parents full of mutual hatred, just as dawn unites the last traces of night with the harbingers of day.

A barren woman is everywhere despised, for egotism leads most men to imagine that they can live on in the bodies of their sons, and they demand offspring so as to remain forever on this earth.

The materialistic man views his barren wife the way he views slow suicide. He despises her, deserts her, and wishes for her death, as though she were a treacherous enemy planning his assassination. Mansur Bey Ghalib was as materialistic as the earth under his feet, as cruel as steel, as greedy as a grave. His desire for a son to inherit his name and dominion caused him to hate poor Salma, transforming her virtues, in his eyes, into hellish vices.

A tree that grows in a cave never puts forth fruit, and Salma Karama subsisted in life's shadow, so she bore no children. The caged nightingale weaves no nest, lest its young inherit its captivity; Salma was a hostage to wretchedness, and heaven forebore to create from her life two prisoners. The flowers of the valley are children borne by the sun's affection and nature's passion, and human children are flowers born of love and tenderness. But Salma Karama never felt the breath of tenderness or the caress of affection in that opulent house standing above the seashore in Ras Beirut. But she prayed in the silence of the night, beseeching heaven to send her a child to dry her tears with his pink fingertips and efface thoughts of death from her heart by his radiant eyes.

Salma prayed, full of pain, till the sky was filled with prayers and supplications, and she implored God, seeking His help, till her cries rent the clouds. Finally, heaven heard her call, and sent down upon her heart a melody imbued with sweetness, preparing her, after five years of marriage, to become a mother and to wipe away her humiliation.

The tree growing in the cave put forth blossoms in preparation for giving fruit.

The caged nightingale began to make a nest from its own feathers.

Poor Salma Karama stretched out her manacled arms to receive heaven's gift.

Nothing compares to the joy a childless woman feels when the eternal laws of nature make her a mother. All the beauty unleashed by spring's awakening and all the bliss of dawn's advent mingle in the breast of the woman once denied by God and now blessed.

No light is more radiant or blinding than the rays emitted by a captive fetus in the darkness of the womb.

April had arrived, roaming among the knolls and slopes, when it came time for Salma to deliver her firstborn. It was as though nature had agreed with her, committed itself to her, and set about giving birth to its own flowers and wrapping the offsprings of herbs and grasses in the blanket of its warmth.

The months of waiting had passed, and Salma looked forward to deliverance the way a traveler awaits the rising of the morning star. She looked toward her future through her tears, and found it bright, for often blackish things appear radiant when viewed through tears.

One night, as the phantoms of gloom roved through those mansions in Ras Beirut, her labor pains forced Salma to take to her bed. Life and death rose to battle one another where she lay, and the doctor and nurse prepared themselves to introduce into this world a new guest. The movement of passersby ceased, the roar of the sea's waves diminished, and nothing could be heard in that quarter save bloodcurdling screams issuing from the windows of the mansion of Mansur Bey Ghalib—screams of one life separated from another; screams of a desire to survive amidst nothingness and nonbeing; screams of the limits of human power in the face of silent, infinite powers; screams of frail Salma prostrate beneath the feet of two giants: death and life.

When dawn broke, Salma gave birth to her son, and when she heard his cries she opened eyes that had been closed by pain and looked around her. She saw jubilant faces all around that room. When she looked again, she saw that life and death were still battling near her bed, and she once more closed her eyes, crying out for the first time, "My son!"

The nurse wrapped the child in silk blankets and put him beside his mother. As for the physician, he kept looking with melancholy eyes toward Salma, shaking his head wordlessly every other minute.

The song of joy woke up some of the neighbors, who came in their pajamas to congratulate the father on his son. But the physician kept gazing with those sad eyes at the mother and her child.

The servants hurried to Mansur Bey to give him the glad tidings that his heir had arrived and to fill their arms with his gifts. The physician remained standing, staring somberly at Salma and her son.

When the sun rose Salma brought her son near her breasts, and he opened his eyes for the first time and looked at her eyes. He shuddered, then closed his eyes for the last time. The doctor came and took him from her arms, two tears gleaming on his cheeks. He whispered to himself, "A visitor has departed."

The child died, even while the inhabitants of the quarter were celebrating with his father in the great hall and drinking toasts to his long life. Poor Salma stared at the doctor and cried out, "Give me my baby, I want to hold him!" Then she stared again and saw death and life still wrestling beside her bed.

The child died while ever more glasses were clinking in the hands of people toasting his arrival.

He was born at dawn and died at sunrise. What human being can compare scales of time and tell us if the hour between dawn and sunrise is shorter than the epoch that separates the rise of a people from their disappearance?

He was born like a thought and he died like a sigh, vanishing like a shadow. He let Salma Karama taste motherhood, but he did not remain to make her happy or to remove the hand of death from her heart.

A short life began with the end of night and ended

with the start of day, like a dewdrop that was night's tear, which was dried up by the touch of sunlight.

A word spoken by the eternal laws, which then regretted the utterance and returned it to everlasting silence.

A pearl that high waters threw up on the beach, and that the ebb tide carried back into the depths.

A lily that burst forth from life's veil, then was trampled beneath death's feet.

A dear guest whose arrival Salma had eagerly awaited, who finally crossed the threshold only to vanished.

A fetus that no sooner became a child than he became dust. And this is human life, or rather the life of entire peoples; indeed, it is the life of suns and moons and planets. Salma turned her eyes toward the physician and breathed a heartrending sigh of longing.

Then she shouted, "Give me my son, so I can hold him in my arms. Give me my son, so I can nurse him!"

The doctor bowed his head and said, choking with regret, "Your child had died, madame. Take heart, and draw on all your reserves of strength, so that you can survive him."

Salma emitted a bone-chilling shriek, then fell silent for a moment. She smiled joyfully then, and a radiance spread over her face, as though she had discovered something she had not known before. She said quietly, "Give me the body of my son. Even if he is dead, bring him to me."

The physician picked up the dead child and placed him in her arms, and she hugged him to her breast, turning her face to the wall. "You came to take me away, my son. You came to show me the smooth path. I'm here. Lead me, so we can go to that dark cavern."

After a minute, the sunlight streamed through the window's curtains and spilled over the two life-less bodies spread out on a bed guarded by the awesomeness of motherhood and darkened by the wings of death.

The doctor fled the room tearfully, and when he reached the great chamber, the glad cries of congratu-lations were transformed into wailing and lamentation. But Mansur Bey Ghalib did not wail or sigh or shed a tear. He did not say a word, but stood frozen like an idol, clenching in his right hand a wineglass.

On the second day Salma was shrouded in her white bridal gown and placed in a coffin lined with soft vel-vet. As for her child, his shroud was his swaddling clothes, his coffin was the embrace of his mother, and his grave was her tranquil breast.

They carried the two bodies in a single bier and walked with a maddening deliberateness, like the heartbeats of combatants. They walked, and I walked among them, though they did not recognize me or guess what was in me.

When they reached the graveyard, the Archbishop Paul Ghalib stood chanting and performing his rites, and was joined by the priests flanking him, their frowning faces veiled by emptiness and inattention.

When they had lowered the coffin into the depths of the grave, one of the bystanders said in a whisper, "This is the first time I have seen two bodies embraced by a single coffin."

Another said, "It's as though her child came to take her and deliver her from the abuse and cruelty of her husband."

A man nodded. "Look at Mansur Bey's face. He is staring off into the sky, glassy-eyed, as though he had not lost his wife and his child in a single day."

Another said, "Tomorrow his uncle the archbishop will marry him off again to some other woman, richer and with a stronger constitution."

The priests kept chanting and praising God until the grave digger finished filling the grave back in. One by one, the mourners then filed past the archbishop and his nephew, counseling courage and expressing their condolences with beautiful phrases. As for me, I stood alone, off by myself, and no one conveyed their condolences to me for my misfortune, as though Salma and her child were not the closest of all people to me.

The mourners went home, and the grave digger stood beside the new grave, his shovel in his hand. I approached him and said, "Do you remember where the grave of Faris Karama is?"

He stared at me for a long time. Then he gestured toward Salma's resting place. "In that grave I laid his daughter down on his breast, and on his daughter's breast I laid her child. I shoveled dirt over the lot of them."

"You buried my heart in that grave too, friend. You have strong arms."

When the grave digger vanished into the cypress grove, my patience and self-control evaporated, and I threw myself on Salma's grave, weeping and mourning her.